The Overlords
of Tlegryth

Jesse S. Smith

❈

Basementia Publications
Silverton, Oregon

The Overlords of Tlegryth
Jesse S. Smith

Copyright ©1995, ©2022 by Jesse S. Smith

Published by Basementia Publications
Silverton, Oregon, USA
www.basementia.com

An earlier version of this text was originally copyrighted in 1995 by the author under the title, "Impure Fiction."

Chapter 9, the short play titled "A Tale of Two Pities," was originally published in *Blue Moon* vol. 10, no. 1 (Whitman College Art & Literary Magazine, Walla Walla) in 1997.

Cover photos of "King John's Castle" in Limerick, Ireland by Jesse S. Smith ©2021

ISBN 978-0-9766423-6-7

Fiction: Fantasy

*This book is dedicated
to my mother,
with love and gratitude
for the opportunity
to write this book*

Contents

Preface

In the summer of 1995, I made my first formal attempt to write a full-length book. The result was a hilarious and wildly inappropriate novel titled *Impure Fiction*.

Impure Fiction wove a storyline back and forth between two fictional worlds.

One of those worlds was the life of a regular college student. The student went to class and wrote term papers; he partied with his friends; he visited his girlfriend; and in his free time, he wrote a fantasy story about a magical kingdom.

The other world was the picturesque realm of the fantasy story. It was a world of magic and excitement. In that world, an enchantress and a hairy farm boy bravely led a rebellion against the evil Overlords who had invaded their homeland, while a wisecracking wizard smoked a pipe with a dragon named Bahb Mawr Lei.

Hey, it was the 1990's. What can I say?

When complete, *Impure Fiction* was about twice the length of the present volume.

Some two and a half decades later, I am only now bringing this story out for publication for the first time.

For the present edition, the comparatively tedious portions of the original book that dealt with the fictional college student's life have all been removed. Only the fun fantasy story remains. I have filled in gaps in the narrative that were originally bridged by events from the student's world; and I expanded a few sections so the fantasy story could better stand on its own.

The result is refreshingly lighthearted and humorous. After the dismal years we have just lived through, between the political situation and the grinding global pandemic, I hope you will agree that some silly, lighthearted humor is exactly what we need right now.

The Overlords of Tlegryth is probably one of the most exuberantly joyful pieces I have ever written. I certainly hope it will make you smile.

~Jesse S. Smith
October 26, 2021

Chapter 1: Prison Break

Cloaked and hooded, the mysterious figure approached the forbidding stone stronghold.

It was springtime in the countryside, and birdsong filled the air as the stranger strode down the dusty dirt road that wound between impossibly green farm fields beneath a bright blue sky.

"Look at those green fields, full of frolicking farmers," the cloaked stranger thought with a hint of bitterness. "They're all blissfully ignorant of the poor prisoner who's being brutally tortured in a dank dark dungeon at this very moment."

The solitary stranger strode purposefully up to the guards at the city gates.

"Here to see somebody," the cloaked stranger declared in a muffled voice.

"Right," said one of the guards, standing aside to let the stranger pass, "in you go."

"Who was that?" the other guard asked incuriously, after the stranger had passed within.

"Don' r'member s'name," said the first guard. "But I'm sure I seen 'im 'round all th' time."

"Yeah," agreed the other. "Me, too." He paused, and then concluded definitively, "Huh."

The guards both shrugged without even looking at each other.

Striding down the cobbled stone streets of the city, the stranger's face remained in cowled shadows. None of the denizens looked toward the robed personage, who seemed important and perhaps even a bit fearsome. Everyone who passed instinctively moved to get out of the stranger's way; even much larger, more physically imposing men seemed to involuntarily shrink away.

"The prison," said the stranger to one of these men, apparently a soldier by his uniform. "Where is it?"

"It's in the basement of the castle, of course," said the surprised soldier. "That's why they call it the dungeon. The stairs are that way," he concluded helpfully, and pointed.

"Right," said the stranger, and there was an odd musical quality to the muffled voice. "Thanks." Then the stranger disappeared. The soldier shook his head in bewilderment and continued on his way.

The stranger was admitted to the castle with similar ease. The castle guards were polite, even deferential, but mostly careless. They all felt they knew this person from somewhere and owed him respect, even though they couldn't immediately place him.

Even the usually suspicious jailer asked no questions as he led the hooded stranger deep into the dank dark dungeon, to the prison cell where the rebel was being tortured.

"It's just what he deserves. That will teach him to challenge the supremacy of the Overlords," the jailer grumbled, and walked away muttering something about an impending execution.

The visiting stranger peered into the darkness of the cell.

The prisoner was filthy, manacled, chained to a wall, and strung up in a stress position. It was clear that he had been kept there like that for weeks, a torment only broken by intervals of whipping and beating.

Seeing the stranger standing before his cell, the weary prisoner managed to ask in a strained voice, "Who are you?"

Without replying, the stranger removed his hood, revealing that the gender pronouns up to this point were misleading. The stranger was, in fact, a beautiful young woman, with rich raven-black hair and shining eyes.

The prisoner shook his head. "I think I'm hallucinating," he said in disbelief. "It can't be you."

"It's really me," said the stranger in her soft feminine voice. "I have come to take you away from here."

"Aswelia," the prisoner sighed with relief.

"My love," said the rescuer to the prisoner as she opened up the cell door and began working on the prisoner's chains. "Come on, Dau. Let's get you out of here."

"Take us, too!" implored another prisoner from somewhere in the shadows.

The beautiful young woman shook her head in reply. "I'm sorry, I can't," she told the prisoner in the shadows. "I used a magic spell to make the guards ignore me, but it's not powerful enough to cover a full-scale prison break."

"Please, take us with you!" the other prisoner demanded. "You must! I can't take any more of this!"

"I'm sorry," said the young woman in a hushed yet insistent voice. "It's too dangerous." She had freed the prisoner who had spoken first, and he collapsed to the ground in exhaustion. She helped him to his feet and turned to leave. "My spell is not strong enough to cover you all," she explained to the unseen second prisoner, and any others who might be listening. "If we were to attempt a large-scale prison break, it would fail, and no one would escape."

"Dau Moth!" shouted the shadow prisoner. "Don't leave us here!"

"We'll come back," Dau said as he pulled away from his rescuer. "I promise," he told the prisoners in the shadows, "I will return for you all."

"You bastard!" shouted the shadowed figure with bitter rage, as Aswelia and Dau made their escape and hurried out of the stone castle's dank dungeon.

Chapter 2: The Racklard Warren

The demigod hardly paused to look around as he passed through the portal to enter the underground warren. Like all Racklards, he was squat, short, and fat, with purplish-brown skin, a remarkably long nose, and pointy ears that stuck up above the top of his bald head like the antennae of some bizarre moth. The doorway he passed through was so unremarkable as to be nearly invisible. Making things invisible was one of the Racklards' best magic spells.

As he lugged a large crate down the hallway, another pointy-eared purple-brown demigod approached.

"Welcome back, Stronting," she greeted him. "How did you do? Do you want a hand with that?"

"Thank you, Venmarya, but I've got it," Stronting declined graciously. "The trip to the market went all right," he told her. "I traded a few shiny stones for this crate full of fresh vegetables and milled flour. Next time," he mused thoughtfully, "I should make a trade for one of those beasts of burden the humans use to haul their goods. Donkeys, is that what they're called?"

"Oh, but if you get a donkey," Venmarya reminded him, "then you have to house and feed and clean up after a donkey, even on the days when you don't need the donkey." With a wave of her magical finger, the crate began to levitate a few inches off the ground, and this made it much easier to pull.

"Huh," he grunted, "yeah, I suppose you're right. Still..."

"So, what's the news from the surface?" Venmarya interrupted eagerly.

"Oh, it's dreadful, as one might expect," Stronting informed her with a casual nonchalance that suggested he did not care much about the news.

"Is it true, then?" persisted Venmarya in a worried tone. "Have renegade Racklards teamed up with evil humans?"

Stronting sighed. "Yeah," he admitted. "I suppose the Council will have to talk it over, and yammer on for hours the way they always do; and eventually, they'll decide nothing," he concluded bitterly.

"But who is it?" Venmarya asked. "What Racklard could be so degraded as to do such a terrible thing?"

"Sounds like it's Boovaus," said Stronting.

"I never did like that-" Venmarya began.

"He has compatriots, I'm sure," Stronting went on, interrupting Venmarya's invective. "He can't have done all this alone."

"Oh, I know," said Venmarya, and it was her turn to sound bitter. "Most Racklards just go about their business; we keep to ourselves in our underground society, occasionally bartering with the people on the surface and generally cohabiting the land of Tlegryth in a basically well-adjusted manner. But with powers as great as ours, it only takes a few Racklards with ideas of their own to cause great chaos in the world, acting as the henchmen of the evil dudes on the surface world."

"So it is," Stronting agreed. "As you may have heard, Tlegryth has recently been invaded, overrun, and conquered by a warrior clan who call themselves the Overlords. These Overlords achieved their conquest with tremendous tactical support from a band of renegade Racklards, led by the despicable Boovaus. Tlegryth's preexisting popular monarchy was hardly aware of the threat before all their strongholds were overrun by the clan of conquerors.

"Now the Overlords are going on a rampage," Stronting continued. "Using Capitalia, Tlegryth's capital city of stone, as their central fortress, they send out raiding parties into the neighboring countries.

"The leader of the clan of Overlords is known as Thradimoor Vizzglyth," Strongting recited, revealing that he had in fact listened to far more news during his visit to the surface than he had previously let on. "This Vizzglyth has declared himself the Emperor of all the lands he has conquered with his ever-increasing army of forcibly impressed soldiers. Now Emperor Vizzglyth is pillaging all the cultivated land and oppressing all the civilized people he can reach, in an ever-widening sphere of influence. Due to this campaign, the Overlords have expanded their territory even as far as the Whett River to the north."

"That's terrible," Venmarya said sympathetically, "but what of the Racklards?"

"Boovaus and his supporters have turned to evil ways," Stronting said darkly.

"I will bring the matter up before the Council," vowed Venmarya.

Stronting sighed. "That must be done," he agreed, "although there is little chance they will take any action. They are a bunch of high-minded self-righteous old-"

"Yes, we do tend to be like that," interrupted a third voice from behind. Stronting turned guiltily to see a shrunken, wrinkled old Racklard standing behind him, an impish smile on his face.

"Oh, hello, Bwenfors," said Stronting guiltily. "How are you?"

"I," said Counselor Bwenfors, his eyes twinkling, "am high-minded and self-righteous, thank you very much."

"Look, I'm sorry," said Stronting with a great deal of embarrassment. "I didn't-"

"It's quite all right," Bwenfors assured him. "You're not wrong."

"Stronting brings grave news from the surface world," said Venmarya gravely. "Renegade Racklards are providing material assistance to the evil Overlords of Tlegryth. We must provide countering forces, to restore balance."

"We shall have to debate the matter in Council," old Bwenfors agreed thoughtfully, "but we're unlikely to take any immediate action. That is not our way."

"Well, in that case," said Stronting somewhat grumpily, "if you'll excuse me, I've got some fresh produce to put away."

"Ah, delightful," said aged Bwenfors in his most cheerful tone. "I do love a nice crisp carrot."

Chapter 3: In Search of a Sorcerer

So enraged was he at being left behind that the prisoner shouting from the shadows betrayed the escape attempt and nearly foiled it.

Still obscured from scrutiny by her magic spell, Aswelia and Dau Moth hurried past the outer guards at the city gate; but as the commotion from the dungeon increased, the spell began to wear off.

"We've got to hurry," Aswelia told the weary prisoner. "The spell is beginning to weaken. Your friend attracted too much attention with his yelling. The guards won't continue to ignore us for much longer."

"I can't," gasped the young man. "I've been hanging from a wall for the past month. I can barely walk. I need to rest."

"Over here," she said, and dragged Dau to a ditch nearby. With some effort, they clambered into a culvert that ran under the road. Securely out of sight, there they rested while Dau caught his breath. They could hear the sounds of alarm as the prison guards rushed about, alerted to the escape.

"We mustn't tarry long," Aswelia said, after the prison guards had rushed past. The twain crawled out unnoticed and set off down the road in the opposite direction, away from the guards. "But we cannot discount the possibility that the Overlords' guards will return," the beautiful sorceress warned. As soon as they were out of sight and away from the city, the refugees hid in some bushes off the side of the road.

"It's not very romantic," Aswelia noted doubtfully.

"Any place is romantic when I'm with you, baby," said Dau; and, cheesy as the line was, she was inclined to agree.

There, they made up for their enforced separation.

"Thank you for rescuing me," Dau said some time later.

"Of course," smiled Aswelia, tying her dress back on.

"I wish," Dau sighed, "that we could have rescued all the others, as well."

"It was too much," Aswelia said defensively. "I couldn't-"

"I know," Dau assured her. "You are so amazing, I'm not blaming you. We're going to have to come back for them. And since we aren't powerful enough to rescue them on our own, and most of our known associates are in that prison, we're going to require the aid of a powerful new ally."

"Emperor Vizzglyth has a Racklard ally named Boovaus," Aswelia recalled.

"Yes," said Dau bitterly, "but I don't think he is likely to be much help."

"What I'm saying," Aswelia explained patiently, "is that maybe we could make an alliance with some Racklards who are opposed to Boovaus. You know, the other side? To balance things out a bit."

"That's a great idea!" said Dau, trying to sound enthusiastic despite his fatigue.

"Although the Racklards are known to peacefully keep to themselves," Aswelia explained, "they might prove sympathetic to the plight of the prisoners. At any rate, it will do no harm to ask."

"Absolutely," Dau agreed. "We should go ask them. How do we get there?"

"That's going to be a problem," Aswelia admitted. "The Racklards live underground. Although they occasionally venture up to the surface world, the entrances to their dominions are a well-kept secret. Contacting them is therefore a serious difficulty."

"Oh," said Dau, disappointed.

"I can think of only one solution," said Aswelia. "A wizened old hermit, rumored to possess great knowledge of history and magic, lives in the great Rendyll Forest, an ancient and mysterious wood which has been largely undisturbed by human civilization for the entire length of history. The hermit is known to the people of the countryside by the designation Oldwise – although that is surely not his birth name. Nonetheless, he may have some knowledge of the Racklards."

Faced with a severe shortage of other possibilities, Dau agreed that this plan was worth a try. "Well," he said, "let's go find Oldwise, then! But," he continued, as another difficulty presented itself to his mind, "walking on foot, it will take over a week to reach Rendyll Forest from here. We could greatly reduce this time factor," he sighed wistfully, "if we were in possession of some horses."

"Alas," she teased him, "horses are expensive, my love; and between the pockets of an escaped convict and a barnyard runaway, we don't even have enough coin to rent one of the skinny run-down old creatures from the local equine rental agency." Aswelia considered the options. "What if we were to steal a horse or two from the Emperor's personal reserve?" she mused. "He certainly has enough horses that he probably wouldn't miss a few."

"Are you sure that's wise?" Dau debated dubiously. "Unfortunately, the whole castle facility is now alerted, with a double force of guards posted at every entrance, and a scurrying mass of soldiers flooding all the entrances and congregating in the courtyard."

Pondering, Aswelia thought of a suitable plan.

"Dau," she instructed him. "Here's what you're going to do. Just walk in to the stables, grab two of the nicest horses you can find, and walk back out."

Dau looked at her as if she had asked him to kindly situate himself just so in a guillotine, then just pull this cord that releases the blade, thank you very much. "Are you serious?" he asked incredulously. "That place is swamped with guards!"

"They're all so concerned with their jobs," she responded, "nobody will notice what you're doing. And," she twinkled, "I will cast a spell on you that reinforces people's natural tendency to not notice things. If anybody asks you any questions, just tell them you're a big general man's stable boy fetching his horses. With the aid of my spell, everybody will believe you."

Dau looked skeptical, but accepted Aswelia's advice.

They walked back up the road to the city gates, where they parted. Aswelia cast a glamour upon her lover and watched him walk towards the danger.

Her heart was filled with love as she regarded him. He was a hairy, rugged farmboy with an attitude. He walked with a long stride, his long dark hair flowing behind him, wearing a leather vest over a loose-fitting long-sleeved muslin shirt, loose tough canvas leggings constructed to withstand the claws of a blackberry patch, and sturdy but lightweight leather boots.

He bravely strode into the midst of the swarm of soldiers.

The soldiers were all so busy organizing lookouts to spot him and scout parties to search for him that nobody noticed him simply walk through their midst.

His heart pounding and his hands shaking, Dau feigned a calm countenance as he walked into Vizzglyth's stables and outfitted two of Vizzglyth's nicest horses with some of Vizzglyth's nicest tack.

"You there!" a voice behind him shouted suddenly. "What do you think you're doing?" Dau jumped. He'd been discovered! He silently wished they'd just walked, it would've been *so* much easier.

"I'm just, uh, outfitting some horses for the General's search party," Dau ventured. He managed to say it without stuttering. He turned around bravely, beholding a battlescarred behemoth pointing a very sharp object at his throat. "To look for the escaped prisoner," he concluded, trying not to look like an escaped prisoner.

"What?" asked the guard scornfully. "Are you trying to tell me the General himself is going to go out on some damn fool search party?"

"Ah," Dau cast about for a reply. "The General instructed *somebody* to form a search party," he answered vaguely. "And they told me to get some horses."

The guard looked dubious for a moment, then seemed to simply accept what he'd been told. "Well, hurry up then!" he ordered, and stomped off.

Dau led the horses back to where Aswelia was awaiting him. He regarded the beautiful enchantress as he approached her, leading their new mounts. Aswelia was tall, with straight shining black hair and dark skin. Her face was regal, though she was not born of any nobility; in fact, her disposition was much more even-tempered than many famous persons of royal heritage have been reputed to be. She had some training in the arts of the magician, although she had not completed the schooling required to receive an Enchanter's Degree. All that school is expensive, you know.

"How did you make them believe me?" he asked.

She smiled. "A magician is never supposed to give away her secrets," she chided, "but I can tell you the principle it's founded on. People have a natural tendency to find the easiest way to survive. I just made it seem to anybody who questioned you that it was a lot easier to believe you than to start a ruckus, and maybe get into trouble for hindering the General's orders. Vizzglyth runs his establishment with fear as the primary motivation. That can be used against him."

Dau nodded. Seemed reasonable enough to him. The young lovers set off soon after the sunset.

*   *   *

The countryside on either side of the road to Rendyll Forest offered little cover. One could see for miles on either side. Dau Moth and Aswelia turned this to their advantage. Since they could see the dust clouds raised by the search parties before those parties could see them, they had extra time to find cover. Four times during the first day of their journey, the fleeing twosome was forced to take cover. On three of those occasions, they managed to reach a clump of trees; but once, no such shelter was within attainable distance, so they were forced to hide behind the hay bales in a nearby barn. Their horses thought this was by far the best idea they'd had all day.

The road they rode on was a broad, dusty affair, and during the daytime passers-by were not uncommon. The springtime was giving way to summer; the days were growing hot, although the first night after their escape was quite cold.

The land through which they traveled was a verdant farmland, long known for its fertility. The grains of the green fields were not yet ready for the first harvest. Seeing them, Dau Moth hoped he would be able to return home in time to harvest his own small plot.

Though they had to go out of their way to find a place to ford the river, the two travelers made good progress with their purloined steeds.

The longer they journeyed, the more they saw testimony of the destructive power of Emperor Thradimoor Vizzglyth the Overlord. Long-maintained public roadside rest stations had been vandalized and fallen into disrepair. Ancient growths of trees, which had been legally protected from logging by the popular government before the invasion of the Overlords, had now been chopped down mercilessly. A few of these trees had been carved into footbridges, most dragged back to the city. Aswelia caught her breath, however, when she saw that some of these proud giants had been simply left to rot.

"I don't understand why they would want to do that," she said quietly, and looked away. "It's so unnecessary." She gestured to indicate the stands of second-growth that had been planted nearby long ago. Conservation-minded stewards of the land would have used those trees instead, so the ancient giants could have been allowed to stand for all time.

The rampage of Vizzglyth's armies had left helpless victims across the countryside. Fields had been trampled, first in conquest, then in sport; livestock had been stolen to fill the Overlords' own larders. Prior to the Overlords' conquest of their land, Tlegrythians had always paid some taxes to their government. In addition to the random pillaging, Emperor Vizzglyth had doubled or sometimes tripled this tax, leaving those who worked the land with only a meager portion even after a bountiful harvest.

*   *   *

The second day passed fairly uneventfully, until sometime in the afternoon they came upon a traveling market. It was a sort of roving carnival, a farmer's market, and a band of gypsies all rolled into one. Little portable shops, usually in the form of horse-drawn wagons full of various wares and advertised by a hand-painted sign, lined themselves up in a town market square, facing each other across broad aisles of trampled earth. These merchants offered enticing commodities ranging from exotic luxury items to common but useful household goods; musical instruments, clothing, spices, cookware, even livestock were available. Local farmers and artisans, aware of the upcoming event and prepared to take advantage of the opportunity, set up shops next to those of the traveling merchants, offering for sale the prizes of their barns and vegetable gardens, the products of their looms and clay wheels, and even the services of their forges. One local blacksmith attracted a line of interested marketgoers with his reasonable horseshoeing rates; his apprentice helped out in the forge while his wife took care of the financial matters, cheerfully and shrewdly bargaining with interested customers, selling the products of her husband's craft from swords to plowshares, and including quite a few surprising oddments in between.

People of all ages strolled through the dusty venues. Some were there to buy, some to sell; most had come to the event just for something to do. The people who made a living traveling from market to market were easy to distinguish from those who, attracted by the prospect of something to do, had swarmed to the market from the surrounding countryside. Of the people who made a living following the market, not all were vendors. Many beggars had found that the crowds attracted by the market were quite sympathetic and often carried surprising amounts of loose change. Of these beggars, most were the stereotypical beggar types: disfigured by disease, disabled from fighting in political conflicts they poorly understood, or simply withered by age, they were compelled to beg for a living by disability or their status as social outcasts. Many other beggars had observed this first kind of beggar and thought it looked like more fun than a regular job; though hindered by no disability, they felt no compunction at asking for financial assistance from fellow festival-goers. There was such a large number of people who were asking for so much in such a wide variety of manners that Dau found occasion to label the whole affair a "people market."

Those who were "on the road" were dressed in loose clothes of a distinctive style; usually well-worn, often quite colorful, always comfortable. Their skin was bronzed and their hair, often matted and twisted into long tangles, was bleached by long hours of exposure to sun and wind. Following a market for a living had accustomed them to greater freedom of lifestyle than any people in Dau or Aswelia's experience; living an extreme lifestyle, they had adopted extremes of behavior. Many were so warm and open that the more reserved people of the country were occasionally surprised or even put off. Others, haggard and malnourished, had tied their lives to the sort of chemical stimulants available from certain shifty-eyed spice dealers. The wanderers spoke their own dialect and even seemed to have their own religion, a faith which few tried to describe in words because of the disagreements this caused. Their religion, notable for a lack of clear leadership, was a tangled doctrine chiefly manifested in the symbols which the vendors sold and the bohemians used as decorations, whether in the guise of jewelry, or actually tattooed on their person. All Dau and Aswelia managed to discern of this apparently popular religion from the vague phrases and garbled propaganda were the notion that it was interested in life and nature, the harmony one should seek within the former and the balance implicit to the latter. Some of the beggars, especially the ones with nothing wrong with them, had apparently found within the collective faith a clause about helping others, and proceeded to tout this idea highly.

Traveling with this fair were a company of bards and minstrels. Their music was happy; it seemed to dance with a life of its own. Those who listened to it became almost entranced; caught up in those frolicking harmonies, they themselves began to dance. The notes seemed to come from the players' instruments with an effortless lyricism. The fugitives stopped for a while to enjoy the music. The minstrels were obviously having a good time; they smiled while they played and sang; the piper even danced a little jig while he piped. Their tunes were so ethereal that Aswelia and Dau dismounted and joined the throng; and for a few blessed moments, two people running away from a deadly force armed with a lot of unfriendly sharp things became just two people laughing and dancing, relaxed and having a good time.

They slept under the stars that night in the wide rolling fields of the countryside surrounding the little settlement which had hosted the day's market. Aswelia had come equipped with warm blankets made of a thin lightweight material, very convenient for traveling. The fugitive lovers wrapped up in these blankets, just a few paces from where they had tethered the horses. Aswelia had quite taken a liking to her steed; she'd named him Klipclop.

For a long time they just lay there and watched the stars. Aswelia saw a shooting star. When Dau asked her what she was going to wish for, she just snuggled up closer to him. He wrapped the fingers of one strong hand in her hair, with the other he pulled her body closer to his. He could feel her warm breath on his neck and in his ear as he groped in the darkness to find her lips with his.

Chapter 4: Meanwhile, Back at the Castle

Grebron Auroyon was on guard duty in the throne room of the Emperor Vizzglyth, but today he was wishing he wasn't.

"They could've made me a cook," he thought to himself. "I wouldn't really mind that job. I might even be good at it!" He glanced warily at the ferocious Overlord, Emperor Thradimoor Vizzglyth, who was raging at all present, regardless of the measure of their responsibility in the matter at hand. "Almost any job at the castle would've been better than this one," he thought wryly, "if I didn't have to deal with HIM all the time."

"This is unacceptable!" the Emperor was shouting. "These strongholds are impenetrable, yet you have allowed a prisoner to escape through sheer incompetence!"

The specific target of Vizzglyth's wrath was the Head of the Prison Section of the castle, a bearded, middle-aged man named Lieutenant Froth. It was not really this lieutenant's fault that Dau Moth had escaped; not only because Froth had been off duty at the time, but also because the resourceful rescuer had used magic to gain access to the dungeon. As it turned out, the dungeon had no magical barriers of its own to prevent access by enchantment. Apparently, nobody had ever thought to attempt a magical prison break before before, so the prison hadn't been designed to prevent one.

Unfortunately for Lieutenant Froth, Vizzglyth never accepted excuses.

Grebron the guard grimly shook his head. He hoped he wouldn't be put on the detail that would undoubtedly be assigned to execute the unfortunate Lieutenant Froth. Grebron had seen the Emperor get angry in this manner a number of times since his assignment to the royal chamber. The evil Overlord never seemed to calm down until he had sentenced someone to some hideous death. This was beginning to take its toll on the troops' morale. Although prospects for promotion were excellent, almost nobody was willing to accept a leadership position, because of the fearsome fate to which this so often led.

Grebron and Froth had grown up together in a cluster of houses in the countryside, small enough that it didn't even warrant the title of "little tiny village." There, as boys they herded goats and picked apples, watching clouds or riding horses in their free afternoons.

When the Overlords had invaded, Grebron and Froth both joined the regional Defense Militia as volunteers. After the Overlords conquered, the fighters in the Militia were offered a choice between a place in Vizzglyth's new army and a place in Vizzglyth's new dungeon. After being presented with this choice, all the Defense Militia attended a very informative lecture/demonstration concerning the use and effectiveness of some truly ingenious devices employed in and in some cases specifically invented for Emperor Vizzglyth's new dungeon. In light of what they learned there, every single member of the former defending army "volunteered" to enlist in the army of occupation under Overlord Vizzglyth.

Vizzglyth was coming to the end of his tirade. Grebron could tell because his contorted royal face was turning a royal shade of purple, and His Excellency was royally short of breath. Grebron was amazed to listen to the Emperor's final sentence on Lieutenant Froth. It was the first time he'd ever heard the Emperor let someone have a second chance.

"Form a company of volunteers," the Emperor said in a voice that was somewhere between a gasp and a shout. "Leave here within the hour, and don't come back without that prisoner! Let him slip through your hands again, and you can be sure you won't slip through mine!"

Vizzglyth extended his ring toward the captive, who bent to kiss it. The Emperor struck him in the face, slashing his cheek with the stone on his finger.

Froth fell to the floor, and quickly struggled back to his feet.

"Get out of here!" yelled the Overlord furiously.

Froth bowed, turned, and fled from the throne room.

*   *   *

"My lord," rasped a dark voice from the shadows behind the dais.

"You may approach the throne," said Thradimoor Vizzglyth.

A squat, fat demigod emerged from the shadows, his skin a particularly distasteful shade of blotchy purple. It was Emperor Vizzglyth's chief advisor: a disreputable Racklard named Boovaus. All the Racklards had strangely shaped hairless heads and protruding pointy ears; but Boovaus somehow seemed even stranger than all the rest put together.

 Prior to his current employment with the invaders-in-residence, Boovaus had served as head advisor to the previous administration; but he had shown them no loyalty.

Upon hearing the news that the invading Overlords were likely to conquer the country, Boovaus had promptly walked straight out of the castle in search of Vizzglyth himself, and offered his services to the invader. It was widely rumored that in addition to keeping his old position in the new regime, Boovaus had been well rewarded with the spoils of the countryside for his troubles that day.

Vizzglyth reflected privately that with a track record like that, Boovaus was not to be trusted; but the disreputable demigod was indispensable: for his magical powers were the key to Vizzglyth's own power.

"That, ah, *man*, who you just dispatched," Boovaus grated.

"Lieutenant Froth," Vizzglyth supplied curtly.

"Yes," said Boovaus with distaste. "I am of the opinion that he will be unable to form a search party sufficiently large to achieve the goal of finding the escaped prisoners."

"So?" asked Vizzglyth grumpily. "What then?"

"In the event that he should fail to raise a party of fifteen volunteers by the end of the hour," the twisted purple demigod proposed, "perhaps the unfortunate Lieutenant should be thrown out of the castle: alone, naked, and bound hand and foot, as an example to motivate the rest of the troops."

The suggestion was perfectly aligned with Vizzglyth's own personal values. "So be it," the Overlord Emperor assented.

Standing on duty in the throne room, Grebron Auroyon was surprised to find himself standing forward.

"Your Majesty," he said, and knelt. His heart raced and his head felt dizzy. Why had he spoken up? He hoped that his obsequiousness would convince the Emperor to allow him to speak out of turn.

Vizzglyth said nothing, but Grebron the guard could feel the Overlord's cold stare piercing him like a lance.

"I request to be the first to volunteer for Froth's company," said Grebron Auroyon. "To hunt down those rapscallion prisoners," he explained hurriedly, "and bring the escapees to justice."

"Hmmm," said Vizzglyth with disapproval.

Boovaus only looked at him; but everyone knew that the powerful demigod's looks really could kill. Grebron glanced away, avoiding the grim glare.

Vizzglyth's voice would have withered violets. "Very well."

In a thrice, thirty-some soldiers had volunteered forth for Froth's search party. None was more surprised than Froth himself.

"I said fifteen!" raged the Racklard.

"Sir," asked forthright Froth, "wouldn't a larger party be more effective? I request permission to take all of the volunteers who have stepped forward, sir."

But Vizzglyth wisely placated the purple demigod's palpable fury.

"The first fifteen shall go," he ordered. "The rest of you, double duty! Now, go guard the ramparts!"

*   *   *

Overlord Vizzglyth's dungeons were damp and uncomfortable.

This is, of course, the obvious description of a dungeon. Here in Tlegryth's capital city of Capitalia, the stone castle's cold dank dungeon had always been damp and uncomfortable, long before the invasion of the Overlords. Throughout the long ages, the monarch, though popular, had always taken pride in the discomfort of the dungeons. There was a good reason for this, if you think about it. After all, the threat of being thrown into prison just doesn't scare people as much if there are plush pillows, and pies and pastries for repast. Imagine the potential dread of a dungeon advertised as warm and luxurious. Feel terrified? It just doesn't work, does it?

But after Vizzglyth and his henchmen had lived in Capitalia Castle for a while, the dungeon quickly descended to a level of squalor hitherto unknown in the kingdom. Much worse than merely damp and uncomfortable, life for the prisoners grew intolerable: a living torment filled with ingeniously designed tools of torture, followed by days alone in dark rooms with nothing to drink, tied to the walls and unable even to shoo off the bugs that bit them. Gives me the willies just to think about it.

There was, on account of his being the only person to escape and the protracted length of time it was taking him to return, a certain amount of animosity felt on the part of some prisoners against good old Dau Moth, our hairy hero.

Of course, it was not his fault that they had been imprisoned, or that they were now being tortured cruelly, or that he had as yet been unable to relieve their suffering. Some of the young men understood this, and simply hoped that he would come back in one hell of a hurry.

On the other hand, there were some who held Dau responsible for their captivity, and reasoned that the delay in their release was inexcusable, especially since as they saw it he was romping about in the countryside, sleeping with a hot enchantress and generally having a good time while they were enduring the torments of a vengeful Emperor who was endowed with a good solid lack of any conscience whatsoever. This view of the matter was not entirely incorrect, although it certainly was not particularly forgiving towards our hero, who was as we have seen making all possible haste.

One of the most bitter of these prisoners who had begun to revile their former leader was a young captain named Blaagstrud.

Blaagstrud was fat and greasy, with a scar across his cheek and upper lip which gave him the appearance of a permanent sneer, an appearance which his cold scowling glance did nothing to soften. Indeed, those acquainted with him questioned which came first, his appearance or his temperament, as the two seemed to fit together quite appropriately.

Blaagstrud had originally hailed from the same general locale as Dau Moth, so it was natural that the two should have known each other in passing for quite some time. Despite this prolonged exposure, however, neither had ever really sought out the other's company; they never became good friends, perhaps because in addition to his unpicturesque looks, Blaagstrud had the unfortunate personality trait of being hopelessly stupid.

The young man so described had joined the rebellion led by our hero after Vizzglyth's troops killed twelve of his father's finest dairy cows on a lark. They were the kind of black and white cows that say "moo," and look sweetly dull, passive and unintelligent while they chew their cud; the very sort of cows which produce the very finest milk: white, creamy and frothy, much deserving of the description "milky."

Blaagstrud's father had come to depend on this milk for his income, until he got up one morning before the sun peeked its bleary eyes over the horizon only to find that a dozen of his prized dairy cows had had their heads and bowels viciously and pitilessly removed. One supposes that perhaps the cows had threatened an uprising intended to overthrow the Emperor, or maybe they were just the most promising large animal for the thrill of a witless hunt. Certainly they hadn't been used as target practice; the instruments of which these unfortunate cattle perished were wielded at close range; little skill was involved; we may be secure in the assumption that the mindless butchering of the poor beasts was not a great feat of arms, proving manly courageousness.

The farmer, stricken by ill fortune in this rather gruesome manner, found himself in the wee hours of the morning cleaning up after the unsightly bovine mess left by someone with a poor sense of humor, when he had been just intending to go about his milking and talk intelligently to "Good ol' Bessie" like he had done every other morning for the last thirty years.

When he learned that his father's cows had been slaughtered by Vizzglyth's army for sport, Blaagstrud had sought out and joined the rebellion.

Aided by his sour temperament, his small, unquestioning brain and his rather frightening appearance, Blaagstrud would have been a good soldier if his opportunities hadn't been prematurely dampened by his imprisonment in a particularly damp and uncomfortable dungeon.

Left to rot thus, his impatience festered and found an outlet in Dau, who had left in a hurry without so much as saying goodbye when an enchantress with a physique to make a prisoner's mouth water for months after just one brief glimpse had simply walked into the dungeon and unbound him.

Blaagstrud's envious lascivious thoughts on what Dau would presently be doing with the ravishing sorceress made him even more furious concerning his own present situation. His anger at times got the better of what little sense he possessed, and in his rage he gave voice to murderous intentions against our hero.

"I," he grumbled, "am going to kill him."

Chapter 5: The Sorcerer's Hut

The vast farmlands ended abruptly. The dusty road which Dau and Aswelia had been following disappeared as it entered the population of giant trees of Rendyll Forest. Under the shade of their spreading branches, traveling was much cooler than it had been under the hot sun. Undergrowth was sparse, so that despite being surrounded by trees on all sides, the travelers felt that they were in a fairly open space, and they could see for some distance in any direction around them. Farther into the wood, as the foliage grew denser, less light reached the mossy ground; long strands of green hairy moss dripped from the trees themselves.

At one place, the road, which was now little more than a narrow cart-path, crossed a neat wooden footbridge over a cool stream. The travelers stopped here to fill their water bottles and eat a light meal.

"So, how do we go about finding this fellow Oldwise?" Dau queried. "This forest sure is big, and I haven't seen much in the way of a human dwelling. Where does this road come out?"

"I asked an old farmer at the fair," Aswelia replied. "He said the road winds through the forest for several days' journey and eventually comes out on the other side at the sea." She looked thoughtful a moment. "I really would like to see the ocean," she said wistfully. "I never have, you know."

"Nor have I," put in her companion. "I'm sure it's quite a magnificent sight, but for the time being we have an important errand, and I'm afraid the ocean is quite a ways out of our way."

"Yes," she sighed, "I know. At any rate, I don't think it's up to us to find Oldwise. From what I've heard of him, if we're to meet him, he will find us. If he's feeling unsociable, we might walk a mere pace from his dwelling and never be aware of its presence."

"You have been informed truly," said a hoarse voice from behind them.

The startled luncheoning couple turned quickly about, but they could see nothing.

Then, suddenly, it seemed as though the shadows of the trees swirled forward, and then retreated, leaving in their place a bent old man, leaning on a wooden staff that was nearly as gnarled as his ancient hands. He wore a coarse loose dark cloak and went barefooted. His frame was crooked, his face wrinkled; his white beard reached all the way to the cord tied about his waist. From underneath shaggy eyebrows, his black eyes peered out, seemingly with a light all their own.

"Are you Oldwise?" asked Dau, taken aback at the stranger's sudden appearance. "How did you do that?"

"Yes," the old man croaked, "I suppose that is one of the names I am known by; it will do for now. If I am not mistaken, I am he whom you seek. As for my appearance..." He paused, looked about and cleared his throat. "You never know what may be lurking in the shadows," he concluded less hoarsely. "Come, let us go to my dwelling. I believe I may help you, and I believe you may help me. A fair trade?"

"It is true that we seek your assistance," said Dau, beginning to regain his composure, "but I fear we have little to trade for it."

"Help may take many forms," replied Oldwise. "That which I shall ask of you is not any kind of material possession. But there is time for this later. First, follow me."

The speaker turned about and walked down a path into the trees with surprising speed and agility.

Almost as surprising as the speed with which their guide walked down it, was the path itself. The young travelers had noticed no trace of it, right up to the very moment when they first tread upon it. Yet once they were walking down the trail, they saw that it was clearly blazed and tidily maintained, as it wandered purposefully through the giant trees.

*   *   *

The sorcerer's cottage was a strange, squat abode with a thatched roof. It stood in a clearing near a brook, with a small garden patch behind it.

At first glance the structure seemed to be little more than a lush, grassy swell in the ground, but upon closer examination it became apparent that the vegetation was actually growing from the sides of the house itself. Moss, long grass, ferns and cheery flowers sprouted at an unlikely angle from the very roof and walls, making the old man's abode itself a living organism. On one side of the cottage a number of strange instruments, all precisely attuned to study lines of magnetism, sun, stars, and other scientific, natural and magical forces far too involved for the scope of this text, were arranged atop a short turret.

The path which the travelers had been following through the trees led up to a round, ornate oak door. The wizard opened this front door for the young travelers, saying, "Please make yourselves at home. There is much which we have to discuss."

Passing through the oak door of the unusual structure, the young couple found themselves entering a cozy, well-constructed maze. A charmingly compact front sitting room was cluttered with scientific instruments, books, paintings, and handmade furniture, all smelling rather more of the outdoors than the inside of one's dwelling generally does. The floor was of earth, beaten and swept free of dust but still nothing more than dirt. The expertly constructed table on one side of the room had mystical designs carved into

its surface, as did the overflowing bookshelves on
the other side of the room. The chairs (which had
to be relieved of sizable piles of intellectual refuse
before the travelers could sit in them) were quite
comfortable. Every leg of every piece of furniture
ended in a clawed foot. The young travelers
instinctively conjectured that a search of the house
would reveal several more small rooms, all
cluttered, decorated and furnished in a manner
similar to this one. Despite its unusual position on
the wrong side of a wall of sod, the room received
plenty of sunlight through two open windows.

"You speak as though you already knew who we
are," Dau ventured inquisitively.

"My little messengers keep me well informed,"
replied the enchanter. "I have been awaiting your
arrival. My existence in this secluded spot is
seldom concerned with political affairs, but the
invasion of the Overlords has caused a severe
disturbance in the natural harmony. Vizzglyth's
armies wantonly burn and destroy perfectly good
towns which the inhabitants had come to depend
upon. I was aware of a thwarted uprising, and that
its leader might be coming this way. I presume that
man is you; and that you, good lady," with a nod at
the seductive Aswelia, "are his rescuer." He
addressed himself to the attentive young lady.
"You have done a service possibly far greater than
you imagined by rescuing this man. The quest
which you represent is the sole hope of driving out
these reckless invaders; and in light of this fact, I
have decided I must offer my personal assistance."

He paused. "I don't believe we've been formally introduced. The people of the area usually refer to me as Oldwise. I know not whether wisdom is an intrinsic quality of age, but the first part of the name is certainly accurate. I am now nearly three hundred years old, and, as far as I can tell, in perfect health. Please," he concluded, "call me Appletree. I offer you my services to whatever extent I might give them."

"I'm Dau Moth," our hero presented himself. "I am much in need of the assistance you offer, and I thank you for it."

"And what might be your name, lovely rescuer-lady?" inquired Appletree.

"I'm Aswelia," our heroine introduced herself. "I liked what you said about Vizzglyth, and like Dau, I thank you for any assistance you might give us. I saw a lot of interesting scholarly equipment outside your house. I went to Enchanter's School for a while but I know little of what you study. What exactly do you do?"

At this point a large raven flew in the open window. It was a handsome black bird with large powerful wings and glittering eyes, well-adapted for sustaining itself in the woods. The bird fluttered about the room for a moment, then alighted on the crooked old man's shoulder.

"This is my pet raven Fluthra," Appletree explained, stroking the magnificent creature, which cawed appreciatively. "She tells me about things going on in the outside world. It was she who alerted me to your imminent arrival. In answer to your question, I observe the stars and meteorology. I am currently compiling a statistical analysis of weather patterns, analyzing the process of weather forecasts. The weather system is of course far too complex to be reliably predicted, but my observations keep me entertained. I also study magic: how it works, and what it affects... and what I can do with it, of course."

At this point Dau interrupted. "What sorts of things can you do? Like, can you see the future?"

The enchanter smiled. "No, I have not focused my studies on that aspect of magic. It is a treacherous realm, predicting the future, for although a seer might be able to predict events which might come about, the future is never fully determined until it becomes the present. Like weather prediction, the chain of events which influence a specific incident are so variable and complex that truly accurate prediction is nearly impossible. Unfortunately, some dwell on this aspect of magic without realizing that it is unreliable at best. When I went to Enchanter's School, a long, long time ago, I knew a guy who studied the future incessantly, and eventually got quite good at predictions. Of course he wasn't always right, but I have known few who were accurate in their predictions half as frequently as he. Well, eventually it started to get him down; he started being aware of all sorts of horrible things that were going to happen at some point in the future. He couldn't sleep at night, because his dreams were filled with the horrors of wars that weren't to occur for many centuries yet, and he knew there was nothing he could do to prevent them. His own life seemed tedious and entirely without surprise, because he knew in advance all that would happen to him. Eventually it drove him mad; he traded his comprehension of what was to come for a complete lack of comprehension, gibbering to himself in a corner or doing strange dances in the middle of fields. His was a truly sad case, for his suffering might have been averted if he had but realized that all his predictions were merely shadows of possible futures. There is no such thing as fate; will power and conscious actions are capable of averting any 'destiny,' of transforming any one likely course of events to another outcome."

"Wow, that's harsh," said Dau.

Aswelia looked thoughtful a moment, then shyly asked if the magician would be willing to amuse them with his mystical powers.

Appletree pondered this request a moment, then said with a smile, "Frivolous display of the abilities one has gained through years of research may lead to undesirable consequences. However, I perceive that your interest goes beyond mere amusement, and therefore I am willing to briefly oblige your curiosity."

Following the old man's instructions, Dau searched the clearing surrounding the cottage for a sizable stone while Aswelia traced an elaborate design on the sorcerer's floor. Meanwhile Appletree leafed through a few large dusty leather-bound volumes from his shelves, finally finding the one he wanted and muttering to himself for a moment. Dau placed the stone at the center of Aswelia's pattern, and Appletree stood over it with his eyes closed, saying words in a language the young couple did not understand and waving his walking staff at the rock on the floor. Gradually its edges began to dim, its shape and color to change, until it suddenly uncurled itself, revealing long pointy ears, bright eyes, a twitchy nose, a small ball of tail and quite a bit of fur. The young couple looked in surprise at a perfectly lively if somewhat confused rabbit which had quite recently been a very solid, stationary rock. While Appletree explained the process of this transformation to Aswelia, who proved an intent student with a quick mind, Dau stroked the creature's soft fur, until it bit him, at which time he called it a damned rodent and opened the door to let it run outside and bite something its own size.

His explanation to Aswelia nearing some sort of logical conclusion, Appletree addressed both of his visitors. "Although masterminding a revolution is an area of expertise on which I have not concentrated my energies, I have learned much during my lifetime which might prove useful in our coming venture against Vizzglyth. Speaking of Vizzglyth, what were things like in his castle when you escaped?"

Dau grinned. "They weren't too happy, I can tell you that."

Dau and Aswelia related the incident of the prison-break, stating the problem of all their friends who were still in a very unpleasant dungeon. At this point, a thought occurred to the hairy farmboy.

"Appletree," said Dau, feeling odd at addressing a decidedly human figure by that name, "in the forest it sounded like your help to us would be conditional, but you have yet to name your conditions. If there is something we must do for you to be secure in your aid, please tell us now."

The elderly magician smiled, but his smile was not a cheerful grin. It was a smile with many years behind it, a smile indicative of an appreciation of hardship. "Dau Moth, my friend," he said gravely, "you are a shrewd young man. I am glad to know that the man in charge of this expedition does not let details escape him, and I am even more glad that you are honorable enough to want everything up front. I do not ask a service of you; my conditions are unrelated to the sort of bargain you might drive with a mercenary soldier, for I give my aid of my own free will, hoping for no more compensation than freedom for all in Tlegryth. When I said that I thought we could help each other I simply meant that we could work together towards a common goal. However, now that you have brought it up, I want you to know that the purpose which you propose to achieve will be difficult. Vizzglyth has enlisted a number of Racklards; not your run of the mill harmless purple demi-gods but heartless purple demons, as powerful as their passive relatives but unburdened by scruples, lacking good judgment, finding enjoyment in the suffering of others. It is important that you realize before you begin this quest that it will be difficult and dangerous, and that you are under no obligation to begin if you find that you value your life too much to risk it. If I were to require a condition of you, the condition would be this: don't back down when you come up against adversity. It would be far better to never start than to leave the task unfinished."

"I am prepared for adversity," responded Dau. "I have been in Vizzglyth's dungeons, and my friends are still there. I could not live with myself if I allowed the Emperor to keep them there indefinitely, and once freed, we must drive the Overlords from Tlegryth, else they will hunt us down and generally make things miserable for the rest of our lives."

Appletree nodded. "Those are well-spoken, brave words, and I see from your eyes that you mean them. Very well." He looked at Aswelia. "Do you feel the same?" he asked simply.

The beloved black-haired beauty hesitated, then decided to answer honestly. "No," she said. Dau was surprised; Appletree apparently was not. Aswelia was looking at the wizard, avoiding Dau's eyes. "No," she repeated, "I have to confess that I don't feel the same. Political upheaval has never been important to me; I would rather settle down and raise a farm and a family than get in the middle of a war. I want to live, I want to be happy, I don't want to get killed trying to overthrow the Overlords or maybe lose Dau and live alone forever." She looked at the ground; she was obviously upset.

"Alone?" prompted Appletree gently.

Aswelia looked up with tears in her eyes. "Can you read minds?" she whispered.

"Not as such," responded the enchanter, "although you might say that I've learned to receive particularly strong signals. That's how I communicate with Fluthra. I think there is something you should tell this young man. I will leave the room if that would make you feel more comfortable."

"That isn't necessary," she said. "You already know anyway."

Dau looked back and forth between them, puzzled. "Know what?" he said.

Aswelia hesitated, then answered in a rush of words. "I'm pregnant. It happened the night of the festival. I know it hasn't been a long time but I took a self-awareness class at Enchanter's School, and we learned to recognize changes in our bodies just hours after they happen." She looked at her lover. "I'm sorry. I know this is a really bad time to have this happen, but reliable birth control won't be invented for more than a thousand years so what was I supposed to do?"

Dau put his arms around his sobbing better half, usually calm and composed under any circumstances. "It's okay," he said soothingly. "I want to raise a farm and a family with you. We'll just start a little earlier than I thought we would."

Aswelia pulled back a little, shook her head and tried to smile. "We can't raise a farm and a family in peace as long as you're a wanted man and Vizzglyth keeps burning down everybody's houses. I don't really want to do it, but I think it's necessary." She turned her tear-streaked face to the passive enchanter. "We're with you, old man. All three of us."

*   *   *

Appletree proposed that the youngsters stay for the night and all three of them could depart in the morning. The young couple accepted the proposition, dining with the old man and listening to him well after sundown as he related some of the knowledge he had accumulated over the long years.

"Wow, that dude's really smart," said Dau as they were making themselves comfortable on the floor with the help of some handmade blankets, generously provided by their host, preparatory to a good fuck and a long night's snooze before the morrow's journey back to the castle. "He totally knows his shit."

"After studying as intensely as he has for three hundred years, I should hope so," responded Aswelia. "He must be the wisest man alive."

A sound from the doorway startled the young couple. It was Appletree, bringing them a lighted candle in the event that either should need to stand behind a tree in the middle of the night. Brilliant though the magician may have been, he had felt no compulsion to invent running water or flushing toilets. Having overheard our attractive heroine's comment, he dissented: "You are too kind, and you overestimate my abilities. I have a vast wealth of accumulated knowledge, but it is all little more than a bunch of facts. All my learning has not helped to improve life for people in general, nor would I even want to advise anyone on the proper life course they should take. I know what has made me happy, but am in no position to advise any other. If it is truly wisdom you seek, the wisest man I know is the Master Storyteller. I was once his pupil, but found I had little capacity for knowledge of the sort he was trying to teach me. If he is still alive, he probably still resides at the seaside, near the mouth of the Whett River. In days gone by he lived peacefully in a shack he built himself on a small island offshore, gardening, fishing, and pondering the mysteries of the universe. If you desire to seek him I am willing to guide you to him."

Dau looked at Aswelia. She was looking at the floor. He knew instinctively that she wanted very much to listen to the wisdom of this Master Storyteller who lived on the sea. When Appletree had mentioned the name he had felt an unfamiliar drive stir in his own breast. However, he was also painfully aware of how long they had been away already, seeking the help they needed to free their friends from Vizzglyth's dungeon. She looked at him, and he knew that she knew it too. The wisdom of the Master Storyteller would have to wait.

Chapter 6: An Execution?

Dau Moth, Aswelia, Appletree and Fluthra left the enchanter's house just after dawn.

There were no stables near the old man's hut. The young travelers had tied their horses to a couple of nearby trees and allowed them to graze for the night; but there was no horse for the sorcerer.

Dau, trying to be considerate, offered his own mount to the elder gentleman. "Would you like to ride this one?" he asked. "The chestnut is a strong mount, he will carry you far; and I am feeling better, I can just run alongside..."

"A ha ha ha, no, thank you," Appletree declined with a polite chuckle. "You shall need your mount, and I shall need my own." He spoke some instructions to Fluthra the raven, who flew off into the woods. A few minutes later, Fluthra returned; and shortly afterwards, they heard the sound of hooves. Presently, an ancient shaggy white pony presented itself to view. The pony appeared to be in no particular hurry, leisurely cropping grass here and there, and eventually sauntered up to the magician.

"Good girl, Rumps," said the old man to the old pony, and began to outfit the equine with the strangest looking tack either of the younger travelers had ever seen. Like everything at Appletree's house, the saddle and bridle were finely crafted by the old man himself; and in the style of the other things Appletree had spent a lot of time on, the handsomely worked leather was visually confusing in its complex interwoven simplicity. Appletree slipped the bridle over Rumps's head effortlessly. Dau reflected that, had *he* tried to do that, all those straps would inevitably have become twisted, tangled, and utterly bungled, and the pony would have run away. The hairy peasant may not have always understood the old man, but he had to admire him.

So they all mounted up and set off down the trail back to the main road. Aswelia rode Klipclop; Dau rode the nameless chestnut he had stolen from Vizzglyth's stables; and Appletree rode shaggy old white Rumps the pony.

Some time later, they had rejoined the main road and were about to leave Rendyll Forest when Appletree pulled up his mount sharply, motioning his companions to remain silent. Dau looked at him questioningly, but apparently Appletree was indisposed to answering facial questions at the moment; so the confused young man turned his question mark eyebrows to Aswelia, who pointed at the trees near the road. Dau peered past the pine needles. These trees, though large, looked a heck of a lot like all the other trees in this forest: acres and acres of them, for more miles than had been adequately explored in those far-distant days. "Somebody's there," she whispered to him.

At just that moment, a tall soldier attired in the livery of Emperor Vizzglyth strode onto the road in front of the traveling companions. He had a long, thin face, and a proud bearing: head high, shoulders back. This figure regarded the three travelers one at a time, then returned his gaze to Dau.

"Is your name Dau Moth?" asked Lieutenant Froth in a booming voice.

"It is," our hero replied.

"Greetings. My name is Froth."

"Yes, I remember you," said Dau Moth warily. "You're the captain of Vizzglyth's Prison Guards."

"I command a troop of fifteen men. We have been sent by Emperor Vizzglyth to recapture you." As he said this, those fifteen men stepped out from behind the cover of the trees.

Dau drew his shining sword. "I will die before I set foot in those dungeons as your prisoner!" he cried, but Froth simply held up his hand.

"Hear this first," the Imperial guard cautioned. "We have tracked you for days, and waited for you to return by this road, as we knew you eventually must. In the meantime, we have conferred amongst ourselves, independent of Vizzglyth and those Overlords who would dominate Tlegryth. We have reached a unanimous decision to offer our services to you. We despise the Overlords! There is no feeling more frustrating than being forced into their twisted service. If your goal is to drive

Vizzglyth from this land, we desire nothing more than to aid you. We number sixteen trained soldiers, not really a match for all the Emperor's armies, but..."

"Well met!" exclaimed Dau, raising his hands in a joyful greeting. "Sixteen may not be enough to stand up to Vizzglyth, but it is certainly a lot more fighting power than three, which is what we numbered when I woke up this morning."

*   *   *

Just more than a week later, the young lieutenant was back in the throne room, where he stood before Emperor Vizzglyth and Boovaus of the Racklards.

"Name?" bellowed Boovaus belligerently.

"Froth, sir," said the soldier, and saluted.

"State your business," blathered Boovaus with bored bravado.

"As commanded, I led the expedition you sent out," Froth reminded him, "in search of the escaped prisoner Dau, of the Moth family from Cholandrasia County."

"Have you returned with the prisoner?"

"Sir, we have."

"Good job, Froth. Bring him forward."

A young peasant was brought into the room blindfolded, his hands tied behind him.

"Is your name Dau Moth?" asked Boovaus.

"It is," replied he.

"Well I don't want to see him!" screamed Vizzglyth. "Get him the hell out of here. Execute him at dawn."

*   *   *

The next morning, three of Vizzglyth's prison guards were walking down a typical castle corridor, not expecting any trouble. These three young men had been assigned to transfer Prisoner 132 from his cell in the dungeon to the torture chamber: the one with the public viewing area.

All at once, without warning, these three transfer troops found themselves beset by sixteen soldiers who alarmingly wore the same livery as themselves: the uniform of the Overlords' own castle guards.

*   *   *

In the days before the Overlords came, the torture chamber had simply served as a regular theater, where traveling troupes and troubadours could perform; and people would journey for half the day just to see them.

Now, instead of a set, the bloodstained stage was decorated with a wide variety of implements of pain. The collection was so varied, it was apparent someone had devoted a lot of time and creative energy to curating it. Who would have thought there were so many different ways to inflict pain? An assortment of metal hooks, blades of varying degrees of sharpness and straightness, spiked balls, and chains were lovingly arranged in a case next to a table, its surface studded with spikes. An ominous wooden frame, twice the size of a man, occupied center stage, dominating the scene like a large brick wall when the brakes and power steering just suddenly stopped working.

All around this torture chamber was a large indoor amphitheater, with its seats in a semicircle, arranged so as to allow the audience to appreciate the painful proceedings.

Vizzglyth, sitting in his box seat across from the torture devices, motioned to the guard on duty.

"Hey, what's the delay here? Where is that prisoner guy?"

The guard said he would return with that information.

A couple minutes later he ran breathlessly back into Vizzglyth's box. "There's a fight in the dungeon, sir!" he said. "Someone has released and armed all the prisoners!"

"What!" yelled Vizzglyth. "Get me Boovaus!"

Boovaus arrived only a few short minutes later.

Almost immediately afterwards, he was followed by a troop of almost a hundred hostile warriors: all escaped prisoners, armed from Vizzglyth's own weapons stash.

Seeming unconcerned, Boovaus waved a hand at the oncoming marchers.

As if from nowhere, a demon army suddenly materialized in His Majesty's viewing chambers.

Chapter 7: A Meeting with Demigods

Fleeing from the ferocious demon army, Dau and his friends managed to escape from the castle.

They set off in one hell of a hurry.

Avoiding the road, they headed for the hills, journeying overland to the place where Rendyll Forest intersected the Glatsflawn Mountains.

Standing on a ridge above a valley in a huge Old Growth forest, Dau and Aswelia looked at the snow-peaked Glatsflawn Mountain range, huge, majestic, and looming in the near distance. They felt dwarfed by the ancient giant trees, and thrilled to be among them. It was an awesome spectacle, with the sun setting behind the mountains: an image far superior to anything you'd see on a scenic photo calendar.

"So," said the lass to the lad, "do you actually know how we're gonna find these Racklard guys?"

"Actually," he confessed, "I don't have any clue. I was hoping Appletree knew some secret passageway or something, but I don't think he does. I guess we have to hope that whoever works for them on the surface world keeps them well informed."

"Hey, why is she marching with us, anyway?" interrupted one of the soldiers, whose name was

Notimportant. "This is an army! She has no place here! Send her home!"

"Aswelia is an essential part of this mission," said Dau Moth. "She must be treated as a member of the army, with status equal to the other troops."

"No!" the unimportant soldier protested. "I'm not going to disgrace myself by fighting alongside a woman!"

Upon which, the sorceress Aswelia raised one hand, spoke a few words of gibberish, and looked the discourteous young man in the eye.

The surprised soldier clutched at his throat and made choking noises until at length Aswelia dropped her hand.

"You really do not want to piss her off," Dau Moth commented drily.

After this incident, none dared argue with Aswelia.

*   *   *

Four days later, Dau Moth and Aswelia were sitting on a log with Appletree, watching a cheerful campfire.

Their small company of soldiers had set up a temporary camp near a stream. It was a good location for a camp: sheltered on one side by a recess in a rock wall, and protected on the other side by a bunch of big trees. As they rested from the day's march, the military men were hunting, fishing, and amusing themselves with a pointless gambling game that involved and five flat sticks and three rocks engraved with certain symbols.

Then without warning, two short, fat, purple-brown demigods with pointy ears and noses unexpectedly appeared in the campsite.

"Please allow me to introduce myself," one of the creatures said politely. "My name is Venmarya, and my companion here is Stronting."

Stronting gave a very formal bow, so gracious that without thinking about it, Dau bowed in return.

"We are here as emissaries," Venmarya continued, "of the High Council of Racklards. The High Council wishes to invite you to meet with them. You may present your situation, and then ask of us what you will. Depending on what you say and how you say it, the Council believes it is possible that they may be sympathetic to your requests; although of course I'm not authorized to make any promises or guarantees on their behalf."

"The message kind of got lost in the legalese at the end, there," chuckled Oldwise Appletree.

"We would be most honored to meet with the High Council of Racklards," said Dau as formally as he could.

"And we thank you most graciously," added Aswelia politely.

*   *   *

The high council of the Racklards was held in a marble room.

Like the entire Racklard settlement of which it
was part, this chamber had been hewn out of the
living rock of the Glatsflawn Mountains by expert
Racklard craftsmen. The long, intricately sculpted
table in the center of the room had been fashioned
in place from the surrounding stone.

Entering the Great Council Hall was one of the
strangest experiences of Dau's adventure so far. He
slowed his stride and stared about him. His eyes
took in first the vast domed ceiling, arching high
overhead, a prodigious feat of artistry. Then his
mind boggled as he realized that the room was
quite full of Racklards, a race our hero had heard of
before but had never actually seen until the
moment when Venmarya and Stronting had
unexpectedly materialized in his campsite.

During the formal introductions that followed,
Dau allowed himself to briefly examine the
mysterious demigods. Their purple skin was
browner than he had expected; their pointy noses
and ears were a good deal longer than he had
expected; and their eyes were on the whole more
numerous than he had expected. Otherwise, they
looked basically as he had pictured them; short and
potbellied, with large, flat feet, stubby legs and long
arms. They all wore the sorts of robes that one
might expect would be worn by excommunicated
former deities. In some ways, the Racklards were
reminiscent of old Greek gods of legend, complete
with a drink they called Ambrosia, which was by far
and away the most tasty and memorable chalice of
liquid Dau had ever consumed. Apparently, some

time in the distant past, their realm, like Tlegryth, had been overpowered by invaders: Vikings named Odin and Thor, who changed the name Olympus to Valhalla.

The presiding demi-gods assembled in this room were arranged around the table in the center of the hall with plenty of room for their visitors. Most of their meetings were conducted telepathically, so it made little difference how near to each other they sat.

Dau Moth was unsure how to greet the Racklard High Council, and looked to Appletree, hoping the wizard would set an example for him to follow. Appletree was bent nearly double, holding his head with his hands, so Dau assumed the same posture, presuming it to be a suitable means of showing respect.

"What art ye doing?" a voice said inside his head. Dau straightened suddenly, looking around at the seated deities. Apparently one of them had spoken, but he hadn't really heard the voice with his ears.

Appletree grinned and stood up. "Begging your pardon, sires. My mind is accustomed to receiving the telepathic messages of much less powerful minds than your own, usually Fluthra's. My mind was just temporarily overwhelmed with a sort of power surge."

Dau was embarrassed. He had just done entirely the wrong thing for entirely the wrong reason. He made some attempt to cover for it. "Your majesties," he said loudly, "we were summoned to your presence. I want to thank you for giving us an audience."

They seemed to perceive his spoken voice, although their reply was again spoken directly to his mind.

"We have personal reasons for desiring the success of your mission," came the thought-words. "First of all, we occasionally trade with the humans on the surface near here, and parts of that trade have been obstructed or obliterated by Vizzglyth's invasion and subsequent devastation of Tlegryth. That would not normally be a sufficient cause for us to intercede in human affairs, but we have received reports that certain of our numbers have joined on as the Emperor's personal aides; and we have reason to believe that, given enough confidence, those renegade Racklards would attempt an invasion of our stronghold here, a conflict we wish to avoid if at all possible. In light of these facts, we have decided to offer you the support of a specially trained tactical unit of Racklards who know how to win battles such as yours."

It was decided that Dau and his entire army of companions should reside with the Racklards until such time as they might mount a joint venture against Vizzglyth. Meanwhile, the Racklardian Special Operations Unit gave the human force a crash course in tactics and maneuvers, in addition to a rigorous exercise program to compensate for inactivity in the dungeon.

That night the Racklards invited the human companions to a feast deep in the mountain caverns.

The exquisite food was expertly prepared, zesty and filling, augmented with sweet, juicy fruits which decorated the table with exotic flavors and colors. Washed down with that excellent Ambrosia, which after a few glasses provided a warm glowing sensation to one's face and belly, the meal was as exciting to the taste buds as the melodies of the magical musicians were rapturous to the auditory senses.

One musician cradled a wooden instrument with eight strings; his playing was melodious, at times harmonious, flowing with a charming fluidity which evoked a smile from the listener. Another played a sort of wooden flute; she played only at certain times, together calculated to an immense yet subtle effect; her playing was fast and provocative, at times almost providing more of an airy texture of rapid notes than a specific melodious line or pattern. Sometimes when not playing her flute, she would sing, her voice a powerful yet somehow distant alto. A third musician patted a complex, syncopated rhythm on a tall, wide drum from which he produced a fascinating variety of sounds. The musician whose notes sounded the most constantly during the performance at first appeared to be a percussionist as well, for he was pounding with sticks on a series of wooden slats of different lengths, arranged in two levels on a frame with a sort of sounding board. However, it soon proved that each of these slats produced different tones, and the musician played these tones, either singly or as chords, in constantly varying yet somehow familiar patterns, sometimes using as many as six different sticks at the same time to sound large, beautifully strange-sounding chords.

It was easy to get lost in such enchanting music, and for a time the travelers allowed themselves to do so, allowing the musicians' unpredictable interactions to paint mental portraits of people, events, and places. Finally Appletree, reaching an entirely serene and relaxed state of mind, thought a thought which had remained unthought at the back of his mind for some time. It had previously been crowded back by more pressing concerns; but with those now alleviated, the thought was given leave to express itself, which it did, flooding his conscience with a piqued curiosity.

"Dau Moth," he said, turning to the hairy warrior.

The young man sat lost in a tranquilized daze, contemplating the music absently, his mind warmed by Ambrosia. At the sound of his name, the hairy farmboy-turned-rebel's more forceful consciousness now reluctantly resurfaced, and he slowly turned to the wizard with a smile of afterglow on his face.

"You told me," the wizard continued, "that when you were in the castle, an army appeared from out of nowhere in the Public Viewing Torture Chamber. Did you engage that army?"

A look of puzzled insecurity stole across Dau's face. "I, um, I'm not sure," answered he. "I guess not. We kinda just ran away. It's a little embarrassing, really; but they were terrifying!"

Several voices up and down the table spoke up in agreement. Nobody wanted their courage questioned.

"When you retreated, did the army follow you?" pursued the questioner.

"I don't really remember. It's kind of a blur. I think they did."

"Who was in the room before the army appeared?"

"Just, uh, I guess there was Vizzglyth, and like, his personal servant, and probably the guy who was supposed to torture me, too."

"That's all?" asked Appletree, disappointed. "You're sure there was nobody else?"

Dau dug around in his mind. "Now that you mention it, I guess there was a Racklard there. Funny I hadn't really thought about that before. When we entered the room, the purple guy raised his hand. I just kind of assumed he was scared of us, but then this army appeared..."

"What did the army look like?"

"It was the weirdest thing," Dau recalled. "There were demon dudes riding on horses of flame; and archers; and, I don't know, there must have been hundreds of footsoldiers, with spears and battle axes. They were the most frightening army I've ever seen. I'm not sure how they all fit inside the castle..."

"Did you notice their shields, was there an emblem of any kind?"

He thought a moment. "Yeah, I think they had large shields made of skins stretched over a frame; and the shields all had a big bird painted on them, in what looked like blood. It was pretty freaky. They had a banner too, I don't even remember what was on it, I just remember that it seemed like my death was predicted by that banner."

A soldier across the table interrupted, "That's not how I remember it at all."

Dau was annoyed, but Appletree encouraged him. "Indeed? What did they look like to you?"

"I thought they had small, circular wooden shields," recalled the man across the table. "They were savages, from some wild country, with long hair and painted bodies, and they wore the skulls of animals and other men upon their heads. Leading their legion was a demon, eight feet tall, with red eyes and green skin, with warts everywhere, and a long spiky tail. Oh, that sight frightened me to my very core, it did! I ran from that place as fast as ever I could, and I was more than relieved when that fearsome host did not pursue us."

Appletree seemed delighted. "Indeed!" he crowed. "Dau, did the army look anything at all like this in your memory?"

Dau looked puzzled. "Uh, no, actually, not at all."

The wizard smiled triumphantly, then began eliciting descriptions of the army of sudden appearance from all the gathered company. Some had seen one thing, some another; all told, few of the stories had identical details, and most of those came from men who had discussed it amongst themselves afterwards.

At last, Appletree asked to be allowed to make an announcement.

"With the help," he said, "of the soldiers who have recently been freed from Vizzglyth's dungeons, I have collected a number of accounts of the event of the army which materialized out of thin air inside the castle. I have developed a theory, and request your analysis, gathered Elders.

"Few of the soldiers' recollections give similar details," Appletree continued. "Many of their accounts diverge, and vary widely. Some recall an army which appeared one way, some another; they recall varied manners of dress, varied provisions of armaments; there are even questions about such essentials as whether or not this mystical army pursued them from the castle. It has come to light that a Racklard was in the room prior to the appearance of the army. My question at this time is whether that army was actually physically brought into the room, or if the Racklard could have simply cast a spell to create an illusion and stoke a sense of fear, making it seem as though there was an army."

"That's some fancy deduction," complimented Bwenfors, the elderly demi-deity. "Yes, it would have been a simple matter for Boovaus to have simply struck terror into the hearts of the advancing rebels, making them believe an army stood in their way. That would certainly explain varied recollections of the event."

"Is there anything we can do to prevent this happening again in the future?"

"Well," came the telepathic thought-voice, "now that you are aware that he has this power, the knowledge can be your protection. If an army appears suspiciously, close your eyes, count to three, then look at them again. Resolute you must stand, and if phantom warriors they be, grow fuzzy and vanish they will, just as quickly as they appeared."

Chapter 8: The Dragon

Appletree the wizard had been two hundred ninety-nine years old for two weeks. During those two weeks, he had felt restless. His help was unneeded in the preparations for the coming confrontation; and being responsible for nothing, he had no means of occupying himself. At loose ends, his thoughts turned to his age, and from his age to the inevitable destination that such an impossibly large number of years must eventually lead to. This was an unpleasant frame of mind, so Appletree determined he would return to a more cheerful mindset by occupying himself with something useful.

Informing only Dau Moth that he would be going on a "long walk, don't wait up," the old sorcerer set off that very night, just after nightfall.

Appletree would have liked to ride Rumps, but he had reason to believe that if he did, he might eventually be forced to leave the shaggy pony on the rocky crags of Mount J'aime Ocha, so he left Rumps the pony there in the care of the serene Racklards, where he would be much safer. Patting the pony on his neck, he took his leave, and set off on foot.

Wearing a thick traveling cloak, he took with him only a leather satchel, its strap across his chest, and his favorite gnarled walking staff: the staff with the agate-eyed head carved from a twisted branch, the one with the inscription in strange, beautiful symbols spiraling around its length: an inscription communicating to any who could translate mysterious symbols what terrible things might happen if by some chance they should walk off with the wrong agate-eyed walking-stick.

Fluthra traveled with him, flying on ahead, occasionally alighting on a tree limb or rocky outcropping, sometimes returning to perch her powerful claws on the enchanter's shoulder.

The previous week, Appletree had discovered a path that switchbacked down the mountainside facing the Glatsflawn Mountains, on the side facing away from Tlegryth. Inquiring of the Racklards the nature of this path, they replied that it had not been left by any of their race, but was probably a remnant of a road constructed by the miner gnomes who had originally hollowed out the mountain's tunnels, in days long lost to memory, before the demi-gods had moved in and expanded the somewhat utilitarian delvings to suit their rather lavish taste. The Racklards had further informed Appletree that this path led along the banks of the glacial river in the valley below, eventually reaching its source on nearby Mount J'aime Ocha.

Reaching the bottom of the last switchback, Appletree saw that he must travel for a considerable distance before even reaching the riverbank. Looking through the thick fog at the cold moon overhead, he heard the rustle of an anonymous life form in the tall marsh-grass and cattails growing along the road. Surveying the dismal, gray scene, he patiently reached into his leather pouch and removed a wooden pipe. Igniting its contents with the tip of his finger, he indulged in the smooth, tasty herbal smoking mixture for a brief but pleasant moment.

Fascinated as he was by natural phenomena, especially weather, Appletree observed the fog on the marshy flatlands he was walking through. The fog was so dense, it obscured all but the closest of his surroundings; but when he descended a slight rise in the land, Appletree could see a kind of pattern in the air. Though it was a cold, damp, clammy night, turning to a grey pre-dawn light, there was very little wind. The thick fog had strangely separated itself into distinct layers: one immediately in contact with the ground, another perhaps as much as forty feet above the ground, still too low to be low-hanging clouds. Sandwiched between these two layers was a layer of clear, fog-free air. Appletree rejoiced at seeing visible layers of air; finding the workings of the forces of nature rendered visible by random chance made his heart glow with happiness.

The weather, he mused, frequently mocks emotions, being all bright and sunny when one is in damp spirits, raining and blustering just to spoil one's cheerful mood. Although Appletree had been feeling somewhat blue hanging around at the

Racklard stronghold, his state of mind was greatly improved by the positive step of taking the situation under his own control. Although the night itself was indeed dreary, our good friend the enchanter was actually feeling much better, thank you.

The wizard stopped to rest for a time at daybreak, and again at midday. On towards evening he finally allowed himself a brief slumber, and resumed his journey in the dark hours before morning.

He missed his pony, Rumps. Had he been riding, his progress would have been much faster. Nonetheless, the enchanter made relatively rapid progress on foot, unimpeded by many of the physical deteriorations which normally trouble men one third of his age, due to a healing remedy he had discovered in a mixture of mold and certain wild roots.

Climbing the switchbacks which corresponded to the ones he had just descended, Appletree noticed a cloud which didn't drift and blow away in the manner of the other clouds. Eventually determining that it was actually smoke, he surmised that he now had his destination in sight, a conclusion soon corroborated by Fluthra's exploratory reconnaissance. It took some time for him to reach the smoke's source, a large cavern behind a waterfall, and the manner in which he was compelled to traverse a nearly vertical rock wall on the way was particularly dangerous due to limited visibility.

Smoke was so thick in the cavern that he could hardly see the walls. Closing his eyes, Appletree walked confidently into the middle of the cave, then cried a polite greeting in a forgotten language. Suddenly a snake slithered past him; a monstrous snake with red spikes all along its back, big enough to be a dinosaur's tail. In a manner of speaking, it actually was a dinosaur's tail, of a sort: for it was not a snake at all, but the tail of the Great Rhasta Dragon: Bahb Mawr Lei, the proprietor of the smoke-filled cavern and the source of all the billowing smoke.

The Rhasta Dragons, a proud race of reptilian fire-breathers, were long ago hunted nearly to extinction by xenophobic barbarians and overprotective men in rusty armor. Tales of St. George's bravery were actually fabrications, a twisted version of the twisted truth. The truth was a pitiless, pointless, paranoid slaughter of intelligent animals who posed no real threat to society.

When he wasn't obscured by his own respiration, the dragon's scales were brilliantly colored red, gold and green. Mawr Lei had an agile forked tongue which he had a nervous habit of wrapping around his long sharp teeth, one by one. His feet were talons, sort of like a carnivorous bird's only twenty times bigger; his wings, folded against his sides when resting, were shaped like a bat's and as big as a jumbo jet's. Although his appearance was fierce, frightening and fucking fearful, his eyes held the wisdom of countless ages; and his voice, when he spoke, was gentle and reasonable.

"Appletree?" said a gentle, reasonable voice from a harsh, deadly mouth somewhere nearby in the dim cavern.

"Bahb!" exclaimed the wizard in cheerful greeting. "I hope you don't mind that I dropped in unannounced."

"Not at all, not at all!" the dragon assured him. "I'm so glad you stopped by. I haven't seen you in, oh, it must be over a hundred years."

"Yes, probably," the wizard admitted. "It has been too long!"

"It's wonderful to have company," the dragon went on. "I hope you can stay a while. I don't get out much these days, you know. Whenever I try to be sociable, even sometimes when I just want a breath of fresh air, some paranoid human assumes I'm a threat to his daughters or cows or whatever they think is important, and they throw nasty sharp objects at me."

"I'm sorry to hear that, Mawr Lei," replied the ancient gentleman, "although I can't say I'm much surprised. Humans in general are intolerant of the unfamiliar. It's a sad tendency, and it's not their only fault by far."

"So, what have you been up to?" asked the dragon.

"I, too, have taken to keeping to myself, out of the way of people," the old sorcerer related. "You see, I left civilization after a bad summer one year, when all the scapegoating townsfolk thought a famine was my fault, just because I study the weather. They burned down my house, the bastards, and they would've killed me if I hadn't, ah, taken precautionary measures in the form of some minor explosives." He chuckled wryly. "Didn't really hurt anybody, but it sure made a hell of a bang."

"Oh, that's a wonderful story," the dragon approved. "Tell me another. All the stories I hear these days, are the stories I tell myself, and I've heard them all before. In fact, you and Kuvries often play prominent roles in my stories." The dragon chuckled. "Speaking of Kuvries, have you seen our friend the poetic ogre recently?"

"I'm sorry to be the one to bring you the news, Mawr Lei," said the wizard to the dragon regretfully, "but Kuvries now lives on only in our memories."

"Oh," said the dragon with great sadness. "I'm very sorry to hear that. What happened?"

"Well, I wasn't there, but it seems he was mixing a potion of some sort. Apparently he thought it would make him wise beyond comprehension, or so I'm told. Well, I don't know what exactly wisdom is, but Kuvries must have put in too much of one of the ingredients, because his potion took him well beyond the borders of comprehension. I think his mind was overloaded with an influx of understanding. There was so much going on in his head that he couldn't do anything but think all the time. When he talked, it was gibberish: little pieces made sense but he couldn't actually communicate his thoughts. He couldn't even take care of himself, but he couldn't stand to be around anyone else. Eventually he wandered out into the wilderness alone, and died of starvation."

"Those are sad tidings, indeed," the dragon said with a wistful sigh. "Kuvries was a good friend, and the friendliest, most intelligent troll I have ever met. He leaves behind an unfillable emptiness in the world."

Appletree was silent a moment, then felt that he had to disclose the true purpose of his visit. "I am most glad to see you, old friend," he said, "and it is a happy coincidence that my business has brought me to the general locale of your dwelling. However, I did not come to sadden your day with my tidings; nor to discuss the shortcomings of the human race, or to mull over days gone by, nor even to tell stories, much as I would love to spend hours with you just shooting the shit."

He explained at length the problem of the Overlords' invasion, how he had personally become involved, and how he hoped the dragon might be helpful.

*   *   *

Back at the cavern of the Racklards, the band of renegades gathered in full force early one brisk morning. Their band consisted of the recently rescued refugees; a few troops who had deserted from Vizzglyth's army; and the small but potent Racklardian Special Operations Unit. This somewhat motley lot, dressed variously in peasant clothing, soldier's uniforms, and Grecian robes, set off without fanfare, departing from the underground stronghold of the Racklards, en route to the stone castle in Capitalia and the unwelcome invaders who occupied it.

Appletree had not yet returned from his sojourn at the time of the army's departure. Dau was reluctant to leave without him, thinking his mystical knowledge might come in handy, but the Racklards insisted that their powers would suffice, and that as surprise was of the essence it was imperative that they depart immediately. Dau never had been good at arguing, and in this instance he wasn't really given the opportunity to argue. It's difficult to disagree with someone who can turn you into a hedgehog.

*　　*　　*

The early morning sun smiled on a quiet meadow in the Glatsflawn mountains, the clouds fabulously painted on the horizon. A doe and her faun grazed on grass and shrubs wet with dew, while nearby mountain flowers waved gently in the breeze. Suddenly the doe startled, looking into the sky at a small dot which was rapidly increasing in size. As it neared, increasing to dimensions of impossible monstrosity, the deer bolted, abandoning their breakfast in favor of shelter.

Had they been aware that the speck was actually an entity who would not harm them (dragons ate fish, reptiles, and the occasional bird, but never deer), they might have witnessed the

unusual sight which now alighted in the clearing in
the woods. An ancient, gnarled old man wrapped in
a robe and carrying a staff straddled the enormous
scaly shoulders of a flying lizard-bird, an airborne
fire-breathing serpent with legs and wings, larger
than a flying steam locomotive, had there been
flying locomotives in Appletree's lifetime. Smoke
wafted out of Bahb Mawr Lei's nostrils; sparks flew
from the enchanter's eyes.

"So, it seems they've left without us," said the
ancient human to the ancient dragon.

The Rhasta dragon turned his head at the end
of a neck of dinosaur proportions and flicked out a
forked tongue. His eyes half-closed, he gently
fanned his wings for a moment, then rapidly shot
out his tongue and wrapped it around an
unsuspecting swallow. The unfortunate avian
navigator, too surprised to even protest, was
swallowed whole in a rapid, fluid motion. Looking
pleased with himself for such a well-executed catch,
Mawr Lei drawled presently, "Choose your friends
more carefully in the future, Appletree."

"Mawr Lei, you have to realize I had little
choice. THEY came to ME."

"I'm just giving you shit, dude," the dragon said
in a manner somewhat uncharacteristic of most
mediaeval characters; however, he really was a
particularly cool Rhasta dragon. Appletree didn't
notice, being preoccupied with his own thoughts.
"This actually gives us a little time to stop and talk a
while," continued the dragon, "as I think we can
guess what their ultimate destination is, and I can

reach that destination in a matter of a few hours of flying, while it will take them days, especially as they will need to take the precautions of secrecy. So, tell me a story, Appletree."

This brought our wizard out of his own thoughts somewhat. "A story?" he chuckled. "Hmmm. Yes, I believe I can probably remember a story or two for you. But you have to tell me a few of your own."

"Oh, there's not really that much to tell, Appletree," the Rhasta replied.

"I'm sure you can think of something."

"Tell me a story while I'm thinking of one."

"Oh, all right, if you insist, my friend," said the enchanter. Sitting down on a windfallen tree on the sunny side of the meadow, he produced his pipe from his pouch, filled it with his herbal healing remedy, and held it out to the dragon.

"Why thank you," said Mawr Lei. He breathed a tiny flicker of flame into the pipe, then shared the smoking contents with the wizard, who proceeded to tell this story.

Chapter 9

Single-Scene Theater Presents:

A Tale of Two Pities

The new masterpiece, as told by

Sir T. C. App'yl Chtrae

Dramatis personae:

Dlyrth: *a nutcase, first voice*
Gwenoch: *his friend the freak, second voice*
A Guard
Rebel Captain Blaagstrud: *a prisoner in Emperor Vizzglyth's dungeons*

[The curtain rises on a bare stage with the lights down.]

Voice in the darkness #1: Where are we?
[Dim lights come up to reveal two men in tunics,
jodhpurs and soft leather boots standing center stage,
facing slightly away from each other.]
Voice #2: We're here.
[Pause.]
#1: That's quite helpful of you.
#2: Any time, any time at all.
[Pause. Strobe light for no properly justifiable reason.]
#1: Um, any idea what 'here' is?
#2: 'Here' is an indicative word, used to denote that
place in which it is spoken. You'll find it in the
dictionary between 'herdsman' and 'hereabout,' and
if you found it there, you could point at it and say,
'here' is here!
[End strobe light.]
#1: And what the hell is wrong with the lights?
#2: Have you tried opening your eyes?
#1: Of course I have. At least I'm fairly certain that I
have. *[Pause.]* That is to say, unless the problem
with the lights is actually a defect in my optic
nerve, a defect which causes me to believe my eyes
are open and seeing strange lights when in fact they
are closed... *[Feels his face with his hands.]* No,
dammit, my eyes are open. *[Lights as from a disco*
ball spin around the room.] Are yours?
#2: No.
#1: Well, open them, you sod.
[Disco ball lights out, house lights on full.]

Voice #2: There's nothing wrong with the lights, you silly git.

#1: [*Protests.*] But just a second ago-

#2: [*Angrily.*] Just my luck to get stuck in some unpleasantly unknown place with a guy who sees funny lights. I'm going. [*Walks off stage left.*]

[*House lights dim, strobe light and disco ball as eight ballerinas run in from all sides and dance in circles around Dlyrth, who doesn't seem to notice. He examines his fingernails.*]

#2: [*Calls from offstage.*] Dlyrth, hey Dlyrth.

[*Exit ballerinas. Lights on, end strobe and disco ball. Gwenoch, formerly known as voice #2, walks on from stage right.*]

Dlyrth: [*Still examining his nails.*] What is it, Gwenoch? I thought you were going.

Gwenoch: I didn't get far. [*Slight pause.*] What do you notice about this place?

Dlyrth: Not much. [*Looks around.*] I think the architects went a bit overboard on the stone motif. I mean, it might be okay if there was some break in it, but as it is it's a bit bare.

Gwenoch: Barren.

Dlyrth: Cold too.

Gwenoch: Damp.

Dlyrth: Unpleasant.

Gwenoch: Squalid.

Dlyrth: A bit prison-ish.

Gwenoch: Perhaps dungeon-ish.

Dlyrth: Quite solid.

Gwenoch: Rocky.

Dlyrth: Stony.

Gwenoch: Potent.

Dlyrth: [*Looks at him.*] Potent? What are you on about?

Gwenoch: Another word for stony.

Dlyrth: But with few applications to dungeons.
[*Pause, during which Dlyrth ruffles through his satchel, removes a pipe, lights it, takes a puff and hands it to Gwenoch, who takes a puff, coughs and returns the pipe to Dlyrth.*]

Gwenoch: Stony.

Dlyrth: Potent. [*Takes another toke.*]

Gwenoch: Kind.

Dlyrth: Yeah, man, have some more.
[*They pass the pipe back and forth a few times.*]

Gwenoch: I think it's...

Dlyrth: Yeah, I think so too.

Gwenoch: Gone.

Dlyrth: Cashed.

Gwenoch: Ashed.

Dlyrth: Dust.

Gwenoch: Ashes to ashes...

Dlyrth: Dust to dust. [*He puts the pipe back in his satchel.*] Some music would be really nice right now.
[*The darkly trippy guitar solo from the end of the Ween song "Laura" plays loudly.*]

Gwenoch: So why are we here?

Dlyrth: That is SUCH a generic question.

Gwenoch: I don't mean to ask any ponderous questions of metaphysical philosophy. I'm referring to our present situation.

Dlyrth: What is our situation?

Gwenoch: We appear to have come to our senses, or some facsimile thereof, under mysterious circumstances. And we're in a dungeon.

Dlyrth: So it seems.

Gwenoch: Yes, but why?

Dlyrth: What?

Gwenoch: No, why.

Dlyrth: Why what?

Gwenoch: Are we in a dungeon?

Dlyrth: That would appear to be the case.

Gwenoch: Yes, but why?

Dlyrth: Why what?

Gwenoch: This could go on for hours. Overuse of this comic motif may tend to stretch its humorous value.

Dlyrth: What?

Gwenoch: I refuse to believe you're really this dense. Look, I'm going to ask you a question. Don't respond with either 'what' or 'why', or any combination of the two. Okay?

Dlyrth: Are we having a conversation?

Gwenoch: Not that I'm aware of. [*Pause.*] So, we have established that we are in a dungeon. For what reason are we in this situation?

Dlyrth: Does it matter?

Gwenoch: Well, I'd rather like to leave, no offense to you personally. It's a bit... damp and unpleasant here. If I'm not meant to leave, I'd like to know what I did to justify my incarceration.

Dlyrth: I don't know. We'll just have to wait until someone comes in. Then we can ask them.

[Enter Guard from the Left and Blaagstrud from the Right, simultaneously. Guard comes on downstage in front of Dlyrth and Gwenoch. They are staring at the Guard, and they do not see Blaagstrud's entrance as he crawls on stage behind them.]

Gwenoch: That was convenient.

Dlyrth: Perfect timing.

Guard: Either of you called Blaagstrud?

[They look at each other, then back at him, shaking their heads.]

Gwenoch: Um, excuse me, sir, we were, ah, wondering-

Guard: *[Ignores him, walks to where Blaagstrud has been pretending to slee in a corner at the back of the stage.]* Blaagstrud!

Blaagstrud: *[Raises his head.]* Yes?

Dlyrth: Wait a minute.

[The Guard and Blaagstrud freeze in odd positions.]

Dlyrth: When did he get here? That other prisoner?

Gwenoch: Shh!

Dlyrth: But that guy wasn't here a minute ago. I'm sure of it.

Gwenoch: Will you be quiet, I want to listen. *[To the frozen people.]* Carry on, carry on. *[They unfreeze.]*

Guard: Do you like it here?

Blaagstrud: *[Looking around thoughtfully.]* Well, it's not exactly what I'd call posh. One might go so far as to say the architects went a bit overboard on the stone motif.

Guard: Some of our prisoners have beds, and drink wine with their meals.

Blaagstrud: Bloody good for them.

Guard: Rumor has it that you're dissatisfied with Dau Moth.

Blaagstrud: What if I am?

Guard: The Imperial Counselor Boovaus is a very reasonable man, er, that is to say, a very reasonable *demigod*. He might be willing to make an arrangement. A trade of services, as it were.

Blaagstrud: I see.

Guard: He has invited you to speak with him. Come with me.

[The Guard tries to brush past Gwenoch and Dlyrth. Gwenoch jumps in front of him.]

Guard: Here, shove off, you.

Gwenoch: Why have we been imprisoned?

Guard: What?

Gwenoch: No, why? Why are we in this dungeon?

Guard: *[Looks them over.]* You two? Oh, we just locked you up because you looked like a couple of wankers.

[Exit Guard and Blaagstrud.]

Dlyrth: Nice chap.

[Pause.]

Gwenoch: So what do we do now?

Dlyrth: We could plan our escape. Or we could sleep until someone comes along to break us out.

[Pause.]

Gwenoch: I am feeling quite tired.

Dlyrth: Right, then.

[They lie down and sleep. Strobe lights, disco ball lights, and dancing ballerinas.]

CURTAIN

Chapter 10: The Death of Blaagstrud

"That was a lovely story, Appletree," said Mawr Lei, lighting the pipe which the enchanter had refilled. "Only, I'm not sure I understand," the dragon continued, passing the implement. "Did you make it up or not?"

Appletree took a long, slow pull from the pipe, then handed it back to the dragon. "I'm glad you liked it," said the wizard. The wisps of smoke that puffed out of his mouth changed colors and formed into letters that spelled out his words as he spoke them. "I imagine that at some point in the future, such a play would be considered highly derivative," he admitted.

The dragon passed him the pipe once more, which he puffed thoughtfully and again handed back.

"I made up the part about Dlyrth and Gwenoch," Appletree admitted. "The actual conversation between the guard and Blaagstrud is largely conjecture, but..."

The dragon looked relieved. "I thought the bit about the ballerinas was a little far-fetched, but I never really understand why humans do what they do. So, what of this prisoner? How much of that did you make up? Did he actually change his allegiance? Is he with the company which is now heading for the castle?"

"Blaagstrud? Oh, yes, he is a very real person: sort of a sketchy dude, if you get my meaning. My suspicion is that he probably made some kind of a promise to Boovaus."

"How do you know all this?"

"I could read most of it in his eyes; it was apparent that his uncomplicated mind was in a state of turmoil, and that he was very disturbed by something regarding Dau Moth. This is, of course, partially conjecture; but I think my conclusions are reasonable, especially given certain remarks I heard him make."

"Why, what did he say?"

"Well, one day before we were contacted by the Racklards, I was sitting near him. I went around the camp invisible sometimes, you know; just because, if they could see me, some of the soldiers would pester me with incessant questions about, like, magic and stuff; and they never understood a single answer I gave them, because what I was telling them contradicted too many of their preconceived notions about the world, so any attempt at actually teaching them was entirely useless. So that's why I happened to be invisible at this time.

"I was at the edge of a clearing, on a sort of bluff overlooking the camp. I wasn't really doing anything or thinking about anything, just sort of spacing out, you know? I didn't even notice

Blaagstrud until he nearly tripped over me, man.
But I got out of his way without making any noise.

"Blaagstrud sat down on a log near me," the
wizard recalled. "He seemed to be disturbed about
something. His eyes seemed to be focused on a
certain place in the camp; I followed his line of
vision, and saw that he was watching Dau Moth,
who was sitting around the fire joking with some of
the soldiers.

"Blaagstrud removed a dagger from a leather
sheath around one leg, and stared at it. He felt the
edge of the blade with his thumb, then cursed
sharply and sucked on a cut. He glared at the knife,
then glared at the circle around the campfire. Then
he started mumbling to himself. I was already near
him, but couldn't make out the words, so I edged
closer. I heard him say, 'Left me in the dungeon.
Boovaus said he deserved it.' At this point I gasped,
thinking I had guessed what he was talking about.
Blaagstrud turned around and nearly cut me with
his knife. I quickly headed back down the bluff to
tell Dau Moth, but on the way down, Blaagstrud
went running past me, knife in hand. He probably
suspected my presence and was searching for me.
Without really thinking about it, I stuck out my
walking staff. He tripped, fell headlong, and landed
on his own dagger."

"Holy shit!" said Bahb Mawr Lei.

*   *   *

Appletree may have suspected, but he could not have known, that prior to his demise, Blaagstrud *had* in fact made a bargain with Boovaus, regarding good treatment in the dungeons, power in Vizzglyth's army, and eventual prestige in the surrounding locale. He was offered all this, in exchange for his subservience. All he need do was supply some information... and perform a favor. A dirty favor, a dirty deed. Indeed, a dirty deed. Deed he do eet? He probably would have, had his intentions not been somewhat abruptly waylaid by Appletree's walking staff.

Blaagstrud did, however, communicate with a Racklard in league with Boovaus; and in those communications, he provided all the information Boovaus had requested, and more. Consequently, despite the approaching rebellion's elaborate precautions to ensure secrecy, Emperor Vizzglyth was already well aware of the presence of the army now marching towards his stronghold. The Racklards had made the entire army invisible, by causing light beams to bend around them as a group, no small feat; but to someone who knew that there was an army on the move, the progress of the troops could be monitored without much trouble: for they raised a fair amount of dust, and left quite a few footprints.

Vizzglyth's scouts were able to monitor the army from a distance, and kept the castle updated on its progress.

Chapter 11: Dragon Fire

"Now," said Appletree, "it is your turn to tell a story."

"Hmmm...." said Mawr Lei. "My story isn't nearly so shocking as yours was."

"Tell it anyway. What I want is to know what's on your mind, not to compare the most drastic events of our lives since we last met."

"Well, all right. You know that cave I live in?"

The enchanter nodded. "Yes, it's got quite a nice location."

"Well," resumed the Rhasta dragon, "this bear found a back entrance to my cave. I didn't mind her living there, I had never had need for that entrance, so I didn't bother her. Then one day she found a tunnel leading to the cavern which I occupy. She got territorial and said she wanted me OUT. I was like, no way lady, I had this cave first. She disputed that, which was simply ridiculous; I was there almost two hundred years before she was even born. Anyway, she took me to court to get me evicted. Thing is, the court she took me to was all run by Bears! The judge took one look at this lady bear, and saw that for a bear she was hot. Well, she flirted with him some, and he looked over at me, and I tried to look dignified but he said to me, 'If you continue to look at me in that manner I shall put you in contempt of court.' The judge never even heard my testimony, he just bantered with the lawyers for a couple minutes, banged his gavel and yelled 'Case dismissed.' Well, the bear she won the case hands down."

"So what did you do?"

"Well, I took to eating coal."

"You ate coal?"

"It burns with a lot more smoke than birds and lizards make. I just made the place so smoky she couldn't stand to be in there, and nobody from the bear enforcement department will dare to go in there, because they can't see me, and I can see them; and I'm a lot bigger than they are, and I breathe fire."

"I see."

*   *   *

Bahb Mawr Lei's tail swished when he was angry. However, a swishing dragon tail does not necessarily denote an angry dragon; even a dragon with red eyes breathing smoke and fire is not necessarily in a bad mood; dragons can't help it, they're just sort of like that. In fact, Bahb Mawr Lei's tail also swished when he was happy, or bored, or hungry, or even when he was sleeping. This in itself wasn't really a problem; Appletree soon remembered to keep out of its way. However, Mawr

Lei also breathed fire in his sleep, sometimes large billows of it.

It had been a fairly dry summer, so there was a lot of dry brush around, perfect kindling for forest fires. Appletree awoke in the night to see that the Rhasta, sneezing in his sleep, had started a good sized bonfire, a bonfire which could well have consumed large tracts of land had it been allowed to do so. Rubbing his eyes, the enchanter mumbled to himself for a moment, then, raising his staff in one hand, he said some strange words in a strange language, almost as if he were speaking backwards. As the agates in his staff's eyes emitted an orange phosphorescence, a large sphere almost as thin and translucent as a soap bubble appeared in the air, then descended on top of the fire. It formed a hemispherical dome glowing with a faint blue-green light, inside which the flames started to sputter and die.

"Hey, Rhasta dragon," Appletree said at the snoring behemoth, "wake up." As the bulky beast exhibited no signs of being about to do so, Appletree looked into the pines under which they had been sleeping, the very trees which had so recently been nearly burned, a catastrophe which most certainly would have been a devastating loss to innumerable woodland creatures. Appletree spotted one of those woodland creatures in the branches overhead, a squirrel disturbed by the blaze, and willed it to throw a nut of some kind. He then willed this nut to land directly in the dragon's ear. The dragon snorted, blowing out a flicker of fire which the gnarled old man deftly dodged. "Bahb Mawr Lei!" Appletree said in a quiet but commanding voice. The dragon slowly lifted his head to look at the magician, then blinked in confusion.

"Appletree!" he said, "what are you doing here? Oh, I haven't seen you in so long!" Then he rolled on his back and scratched his gargantuan body, from the top of his neck to the bottom of his tail. Rolling on his scaly back, he arched his spine and stretched his claws. "Hmmm," he mused to himself, "I feel as if I flew a long distance yesterday." Then, rolling back over and squatting in his normal waking position, he looked at Appletree; the wizard could visibly watch the dragon's process of remembering as Mawr Lei was confronted with all that his Short Term had recently dumped into Long Term.

"Sorry, I'm kinda groggy in the morning. Why did you wake me up?"

"Good morning, Bahb Mawr Lei. You, ah, sleep with the thermometer cranked up to 'full,'" Appletree wryly observed, pointing to the glowing coals underneath the glowing blue hemisphere.

"What happened?"

"Oh, it looks like you sneezed."

"Dreadfully sorry, my allergies do get bad in this season."

"Your sneeze nearly burned down the forest."

If you've never seen a dragon look embarrassed, it may be difficult to picture the expression which now played upon Mawr Lei's features. "That's why I sleep in a stone cave. How did you put it out?"

"Oh, you know, just a force field to stop air circulation. Burn itself out, smother it you see."

The dragon nodded. He didn't see, but it was too early in the morning to worry about it. Early in the morning? No, the sun wasn't even beginning to show, it was still late at night. "What does palpate mean?" he asked.

"What?"

"Do you ever wake up with a word in your head, and, like, somebody in a dream was tossing it around, but you can't really remember what it means?"

"Well, according to Webster, it means to 'to examine by touching, as for medical diagnosis.'"

"Huh," Bahb acknowledged. "Okay, well, thanks."

"I'm afraid," Appletree continued wryly, "we're going to have to relocate camp to a less combustible site."

"Now?" said Mawr Lei; nonetheless he offered his back to the magician, who majestically levitated off the ground and landed precisely situated. "Wow," the Rhasta commented as he unfurled his prodigious wings and waved them to produce an updraft of tremendous force, lifting himself and his passenger off the ground in an incomparable rush, "I'm impressed."

"I practiced that move," Appletree confessed, watching the ground as it fell farther and farther away with mind-numbing rapidity.

*   *   *

Appletree and Mawr Lei alighted on a glacier. They had been flying for hours, and the dragon was exhausted. It was too cold, there at the top of the high mountain pass, to set up much of a camp. The giant dragon, internal furnaces combusting to keep his body warm, rolled up in a ball on the glacier's surface; Appletree was obliged to lie on top of him for warmth, all wrapped up in his homemade cloak.

Huddled in this rather intimate position, the dragon was not afraid to ask the enchanter, "So, how do you feel about your involvement in all this?"

Appletree tugged on his long beard and answered, "To tell you the honest truth, I feel like I volunteered to fill a position, sacrificed to make myself available, and then found out they don't want me. When Dau Moth returned to Vizzglyth's castle for his friends, I got stuck taking care of the horses, because they thought they could take him by surprise and therefore didn't require my assistance. Then when the army was in training with the Racklard Special Operations Unit, I felt so... useless. The things I study have no bearing on the things they were trying to accomplish. I use magic for entirely different purposes. Those demi-gods know so much more about it than I do, they know more about everything than I do, being immortal demi-gods. I got sick of watching, so I just wandered around aimlessly until I finally left to come look for you. You know what I found when I returned."

"I think volunteering to help was the honorable thing to do," said the Rhasta reassuringly.

"Thank you. But now I think of my poor garden. So much good fruit rotten on the vine, my poor strawberries absolutely strangled with weeds and parched with thirst. This is the first time in over a century that I've been away from my home for so long. I'm fairly certain I didn't adequately prepare my home for my departure prior to that event. I will be certain of it when I return to find the whole place all in a shambles from my pets."

"Oh, you have pets!" said the dragon excitedly. "I've never been able to keep pets around for very long."

Just as he said that, it occurred to Appletree that he had not seen Fluthra since shortly after his reunion with Bahb Mawr Lei. *Well*, he thought, *I'm sorry I led that faithful bird to its death.* Now Appletree told the dragon about his pets, tactfully omitting the missing raven from the list, which included a surprising number of animals.

"So you see," the wizard concluded, "in my absence, every one of these animals will overrun my house. They know how to get in, and without me to entertain them I fear they may well entertain themselves by playing with my scientific equipment. They simply have no respect for property."

"Wow," said the Rhasta dragon, "you just said a mouthful, my friend. The implications of your last statement... you could write a book about them. Although such a book would probably deal a lot with politics or philosophy; or perhaps the philosophy of politics, or maybe something even more obscure than that..." Bahb Mawr Lei had a secret passion for historical novels. In the dragon culture, books were published in the form of bronze sheets which some unfortunate dragon had inscribed by hand, or, rather, by talon in this case.

Mawr Lei had a flash of inspiration. He could write a book, a novel about this conflict, with himself and Appletree as central characters! His novel would have to demonstrate that it was nature's way to have no respect for property. Not that he personally was advocating some radical cause; actually he was adamant about considering as decidedly HIS the cavern where he resided and certain valuables and keepsakes therein including, known only to the dragon himself, quite a few gems of such monstrous size that the value of a single one was greater than the entire yearly expenditures of a small kingdom.

Mawr Lei started daydreaming about where he could procure a large quantity of bronze, then began to outline the story in his head.

Chapter 12: The Novel

Here it should be noted that Bahb Mawr Lei's famous historical novel *The Silkscreen of Life* was used as the basis for much of the present text. As any scholar can attest, Tlegryth was a pretty obscure country. Few historical resources exist to tell its tale, for not a lot was ever written about it, or even in it. Mawr Lei's historical novel has thus provided much assistance and information that was necessary to the present author.

The ungainly original bronze tablets of Mawr Lei's completed text weighed well over five hundred pounds. Perhaps this is why he was unable to find a publisher.

The disappointed dragon one evening overindulged in a certain root, then popular with mystics and their friends, which grew in the mountains surrounding his cavern; and flew off into the unknown. He never again returned to the cave which up until that point he had occupied continuously for almost three hundred years. It is unlikely that he was physically hurt, for dragons are remarkably hardy creatures. It is far more likely that he got lost and eventually found another home somewhere else.

Appletree's memoirs suggest that the dragon may have taken to living underwater; and although he offered no direct evidence to support this hypothesis, there is no reason to discount his testimony. After all, Appletree knew Bahb Mawr Lei better than ever mortal knew dragon; and as such, Appletree was aware of the little-known fact that dragons can breathe underwater. Furthermore, as a young dragon larvae Mawr Lei had fantasized about one day being a ferocious deep sea dragon. He pictured himself jumping out from behind rocks and scaring whales.

Meanwhile, the Rhasta's manuscript, the only known halfway accurate history of Tlegryth, was abandoned in his empty cave. The damp air from the waterfall turned the bronze green; moss grew in the cavern's mouth; and the space gradually acquired the malodorous, unwashed smell of hibernating bears. The tablets might have perished in unread obscurity were it not for the greatest of human virtues: lust.

Yes, lust, I say, is a great virtue: for it provides entertainment, propagates the species, and has served as a muse for countless poets, artists and novelists throughout history.

Granted, evil has been done in the name of lust; and yet, we would remind the reader that evil has also been done in the name of the gods, likely including whatever God the reader holds most dear. In both cases, this is not due to the nature of that in the name of which the actions were done, but to the nature of the doers: misguided psychopaths and politicians around the world and throughout history. That was my little soapbox for today.

Lust, the greatest of virtues, had blessed a young couple with the gift of creativity. Instead of building a shrine to lust, as most folks do when they are blessed by something, these kids went off to find a place where they could fulfill their lust passionately, noisily, and safe from disturbance.

Hans and Greta, breathless, sweaty, and horny as hell, found a place where once, centuries ago, a waterfall had flowed over the mouth of a cavern, blocking it from outside view. A landslide had changed the course of the glacial flow, leaving the cavern open to air. The twain carefully picked their way down a pile of rubble, and alighted on the mossy floor of the cavern.

"Ja," said Greta. "Oh, this is a nice place."

It was, indeed, a very nice place, and the lovers were very nice to each other while they were there.

Afterwards, adventurous Hans decided to take a look around. When he found Bahb Mawr Lei's stash of gems he got even more excited than he had been when Greta... I'll leave that to your imagination.

Hans and Greta, consequently, became exceedingly rich.

At a later date, they hired some workers to assist with the removal of some troublesome, annoyingly heavy bronze tablets, behind which they believed were hidden the greatest treasures in the entire dragon hoard. They were wrong, of course; the best specimens from Mawr Lei's stash were more cleverly concealed than that.

Failing to recognize the true value of the giant bronze tablets, Hans and Greta were about to melt them down for scrap when the town metalsmith called their attention to the strange markings scratched into both sides of each ungainly piece of metal.

Hans had no interest in such foofy tomfoolery, for he considered such things basically irrelevant. But just before the tablets were destroyed forever, Greta brought them to the attention of the local priest: a wise and learned man, well-loved and respected by all the townsfolk. As it happened, this particular priest's sermons generally dwelt more on the nature of kindness and the pursuit of happiness than on guilt, sin, and the torments of hellfire. He was known as Father Auld Wheiz, and it was widely rumored that he was the oldest man ever to have lived. Had anyone known to what extent this rumor was correct, they would have burned him for sorcery.

Thus it came to pass that Appletree translated Bahb Mawr Lei's book, centuries after the dragon wrote it; and then the rather unwieldy original manuscript was melted down for scrap. The priestly translation (into Latin, of course) was itself nearly lost when our beloved magician passed away at last. Fortunately, his belongings were not destroyed; they were simply left in his attic.

More centuries passed before a leather-bound tome was retrieved from the dusty attic by young Johann Eichmann, who saw it by chance one day and liked the design embossed into the front cover.

The boy's father, who just happened to study ancient Latin, made yet another translation into modern German. He was at last successful in doing something that would have made the manuscript's fire-breathing original author overjoyed: he got it published. That publication was translated again into many language, and widely distributed to college libraries the world 'round.

Thus it is thanks to both diligent scholarship and incidents of pure random chance that I am able to present the remaining events which conclude this strange tale.

Chapter 13: March of the Rebels

Dau Moth did not want to attack Vizzglyth without backing from Appletree. Where could the magician be?

The young agriculturist-turned-warrior reminded himself that the wizard could take care of himself.

The Racklards had insisted that their powers far exceeded the magician's, and that therefore his absence was not of particular concern; nonetheless, the kind, wise old man had a mannerism about him which bespoke qualities which the ostracized former deities somehow lacked; a vivaciousness, a certain sense of originality which made his eyes bright beneath the shadows of his bushy eyebrows.

Dau pushed the slop around on his plate. Soldiers' fare. Only the extreme hunger occasioned by the long day's march persuaded his stomach to accept such unappetizing morsels. He remembered how much better meals had seemed with Appletree around, and now deemed it certain that the mischievous old man had changed the water into wine at every repast.

The Racklardian Special Operations Unit had briefed them not an hour before, informing the

assembled troops of their plan to recapture
Tlegryth from the false Emperor Vizzglyth. He
occupied a fortress at the geographical center of the
country. This fortress stood on a hill which
provided a commanding view of the surrounding
countryside. The hill was at the tip of the
triangular piece of land in the middle of a Y-shaped
intersection of two rivers, effectively a natural
moat. The city of Capitalia had grown near the
castle, encouraged by the protection, the irrigation,
and the obvious commercial benefits of this
location. All the land for miles around had been
cultivated, which served multiple purposes of
feeding the people of Capitalia, providing them with
goods to barter, and surrounding the castle with
land which provided no cover for an advancing
army.

The rebel army was, of course, invisible, which
would provide an element of surprise which would
be a necessary factor in taking the castle. They
were marching a direct route between the
Glatsflawns and the castle, so that a river crossing
would be unnecessary. The Racklards proposed to
lead the company straight through Capitalia and up
to the castle wall. In the event that the castle gate
was open, the whole company could simply march
through. If it was not, three humans could be
levitated over the wall to rectify the situation.
Either way, the plan seemed fairly straightforward;
invisibility was a great aid in taking a castle by
surprise, and their intensive training from the
demi-gods had taught them the necessary skills and

finer points of hand to hand sword combat. Troops were reminded of certain maneuvers and tactics, and enjoined to do their best to unseat the tyrannical despot.

Dau thought the plan seemed logical, but it lacked sparkle. It wasn't the stuff of a Homeric poem, with troops hidden inside a wooden horse. He would have preferred to have the Racklards levitate livestock over the castle walls to distract the guards while some of the soldiers snuck around and stole everybody's weapons. But the purple captains would have none of his suggestions, saying that only a mortal would waste a thought on such an extravagant scheme. His pride a little offended, Dau sat apart from his companions and watched the fire, quietly lost to his own thoughts.

At a time when he felt that his mind should be occupied with nothing but the present, to keep from fretting about the morrow's altercation, Dau found that he could think of nothing but the future. Fortunately he found he was not too distressed at the prospect of the coming battle; it would be won or lost, and his worrying would affect the outcome little. No, what concerned our hero at this moment was the possibility that their effort might succeed. Until this moment he had given it little thought; he now recognized this as poor prior planning. Who should rule Tlegryth, if he and his fellow rebels won the next day's fight? There had been a monarchy ruling the country prior to the Overlords' invasion, but the invaders had executed that monarch. Since that time no less than six young men had claimed to

be the king's first-born son. All were of
approximately the same age; their six separate
mothers all claimed to have been the king's
mistress. Perhaps they were all telling the truth.
This didn't really stir any sense of obligation in our
hero's breast, as none of the king's alleged offspring
had joined with the rebel forces, contenting
themselves instead to argue with each other about
their ages. Dau had not fought as hard as he had
only to turn the country over to such people.
Actually, now that he thought of it, Dau hadn't been
fighting FOR anybody; his struggle had been
AGAINST Vizzglyth.

No, on second consideration, this wasn't
entirely true. He'd been fighting for himself. But
that didn't necessarily mean... Images of himself in
the royal Throne of Tlegryth faded in and out of his
consciousness. Dau wasn't sure he really desired to
live the life of a politician; the more quiet, rustic life
he had envisioned for himself with Aswelia traded
places with the picture of himself on the throne; he
saw himself on an overstuffed chair near the fire in
his cozy country living room. Dau found himself in
a sort of swirling realm of possibility. Nothing was
definite in this zone of reality; everything was
possible, and could be consciously created, but such
images never lasted long, always swirling away into
other images, other possibilities, a confusing
eternal swarm of them. After watching the meat on
his plate get up and gnaw a piece of wilted lettuce,
he determined that tonight someone had turned the
water into something a lot stronger than wine. This

turned his mind back to thoughts of Appletree; the old man would have been a perfect companion for such an experience. Dau suddenly thought of another reason why he wished the enchanter could have been there for the attack: Appletree would have been an ideal candidate for the next ruler of Tlegryth. The old man would be a fair and impartial judge to every case brought before him, would neither overtax nor overbudget, would always be honest to the common people of the land.

Dau sought out Aswelia, to get her opinion of his idea. She was on the other side of the fire, joking with some of her fellow soldiers. When she saw him she burst out laughing for no apparent reason.

"General!" she cried. "The Racklards put distilled Ambrosia root in our dinners!"

Dau, fancying his sweetheart to have suddenly grown four extra eyes, reported his meditations to her. She agreed and congratulated him for the idea.

Chapter 14: The Battle of Capitalia

The next morning the rebel army, energized by the caffeinated, analgesic root the Racklards had mixed with breakfast, stood in the middle of a lettuce field, preparing to rush into the city. The morning light painted the sky in pastels; morning clouds hung thick overhead, clouds of the variety which generally (but don't always) burn off by lunchtime. Dau Moth clutched his sword, trying not to think of the possibility that he might have to actually use it soon, perhaps to bloody and gruesome ends. He was thus not paying attention when the signal was given to commence the charge, but he figured it out when everybody else started running.

Capitalia had wide streets paved with cobblestones, which the invaders rushed down. Some of the buildings in the city were of vast proportions; they towered above the city streets, spires of varying heights jutting at odd angles from their extremities. The rebels passed a domed temple, its entire surface carved with intricately worked designs. Patterns of intertwining carved vines twisted with infinite complexity, eventually becoming more abstract than representational, up to a giant eyeball perched with seeming precariousness on the apex. Apparently the workmen who constructed these ornate edifices had intended that they be enjoyed by generations of their descendants. Those good people would have shuddered to see their creations now. Although the structures themselves had not been damaged, the benevolent, exultant spirit which had inspired their construction was now hideously degraded by the twisted purposes they now served. Executed bodies were publicly exhibited, strung up at intervals around exteriors; some of them appeared to have been not only killed but horribly mutilated in the process.

Although you, dear reader, have been allowed glimpses of the sorts of things that go on inside Capitalia Castle, you've never actually seen the structure itself from the outside.

The castle was situated at the top of a rocky protuberance at the far end of the city. It was constructed from the same basaltic rock on which it stood. It had an irregular outline: angular and spacious, the structure hadn't been built all at once, but rather had been accumulated by succeeding generations of architects, many of whom had varying ideas concerning the proper shape for a castle. Nonetheless it was quite a solid affair, with three tall, threatening and quite phallic towers positioned randomly about its bulk, a forbidding sight to any who aspired to invade it; in this respect if in no other it was an architectural success.

As the band of outlaws approached this structure they perceived that it had been walled in by a battlemented barricade complete with watchtowers and protected walkways at the top from which archers could launch their projectiles, an armada of arrows, without exposing themselves to any danger posed by the would-be invaders. This barricade had been recently constructed, down the hill from the castle to provide those inside with a double barrier. Vizzglyth had been warned and was expecting the expedition.

*   *   *

When he saw the barricade, Dau couldn't understand why the Racklardian Special Operations Unit had allowed the attack to proceed as planned when clearly their plans should have been revised to account for this new development. However, he soon noticed that the air near the barricade was shimmering, sending out little jolts of static electricity; evidently some great stress was occurring, mostly imperceptible to the human eye. Dau quickly guessed at what had happened: the Racklardian Special Operations Unit had met with unexpected resistance in the form of Racklards in league with Boovaus. The resulting altercation had prevented the sending of any sign which might have warned the human troops. Indeed, as the bewildered humans watched, smoke began to billow out of a point in the air nowhere near anything worth mention but directly between the battlements on the barricade and the ground. The smoke showed no signs of abating; contrariwise, it poured out of empty air in a general abundance as if, like the common housefly, it were in no short supply. As it continued in this manner, the shimmering and electrical disturbances in the air increased in proportion until with an audible groan and a pop energy was diverted from invisibility and two groups of fiercely determined Racklards suddenly appeared, both now putting all the energy they could muster into some kind of showdown, a contest of strength, to either fortify the barricade or destroy it.

*   *   *

Just because something isn't mentioned in a story, doesn't mean it didn't happen. Speaking as the author, I presume we can all take it for granted that everyone in the army has been eating and relieving themselves with some regularity; therefore no explicit detailed descriptions are particularly necessary where they're not relevant to the plot. Often there is so much to tell that space considerations preclude the inclusion of stuff that isn't essential to the plot. Not that this particular story necessarily functions along those lines. In fact, let's face it, most of the stuff included herein is far from essential information.

In every river in every story you've ever read, there were a thousand little fish, hiding behind a thousand little rocks, roots and banks, eating bugs and each other a thousand miles downriver from the action. Such fish should by rights remain anonymous, as they are basically irrelevant to the storyline. It's really too bad, because I would so badly like to introduce you to Harold the trout. Instead I will content myself with giving you further information concerning Grebron Auroyon, former guard for Emperor Vizzglyth, now a soldier fighting with Dau and the Racklardian Special Operations Unit.

Throughout all this time that I've been babbling about Appletree and Bahb Mawr Lei, good Grebron Auroyon has been trooping along, marching towards Tlegryth's Castle Capitalia with his companions, uncomplainingly choking down the slightly slimy slop served him instead of food.

Now, while the human attackers on the ground and the human defenders on the barricade watched the Racklardian showdown, both groups convinced of their own powerlessness when compared to the powers of the demi-gods, Grebron had an idea. He was a man of action, and he couldn't bear the inaction of watching someone else fight a battle he had a stake in. One implication of the Racklardian standoff was that he was no longer invisible, but seeing that Vizzglyth's guards atop the barricade had their attention absorbed by the power surge from the superpowers, Grebron approached the barricade. It was a sturdy, imposing fence, not very inviting to potential climbers, but climbing wasn't the idea he had right now. He was hoping he had successfully learned a trick that the magician

Appletree had tried to teach him. Appletree had at one time attempted to teach a seminar on useful skills to a group of soldiers who considered themselves capable and interested; however, most of them showed little capacity for or interest in the sort of things the old magician had been trying to impart. Grebron had taken a fancy to the things the old man had been lecturing about, and though too shy to approach him personally and request further tutoring, had nonetheless practiced in his own quarters the skills Appletree had discussed at the workshop. Now he hoped he had perfected a certain trick he had seen Appletree perform on a number of occasions. Grebron concentrated on the end of his finger, willing the power which holds the universe together to use his fingertip as a focal point. He held his finger close to the wall and concentrated, concentrated, concentrated. Finally he felt heat on his face and allowed his eyes to open. Startled by the blue flame on his fingertip, he shook it off his hand without thinking. No matter, he had started the wall smoldering. Blowing on the flames he encouraged them, cheered on by his friends who had noticed what he was doing. It was however unfortunate for him that they noticed, for their cries brought the attention of the castle guards, who were less encouraging. Grebron got out of their range with an arrow in his posterior as a reward for his courage. In those days, the removal of arrowheads was performed with little delicacy. He had, however, started a blaze in the barricade wall which, if not dealt with soon, could pose a serious threat to those standing atop it.

*   *   *

That would have been a nice way for a common soldier to have claimed a larger part in the battle, but it didn't take Vizzglyth's soldiers long to put out the fire Grebron started at so dear a price. However, Grebron himself never knew this, for he passed out, and when he regained consciousness, the wall was a smoking ruins. We'll let him delude himself, because he deserves it for being so courageous, but here's what really happened.

*   *   *

A matter of minutes after Grebron started the fire, the guards on top of the barricade had put it out. However, it did divert everyone's attention away from the battle between the Racklards for a moment. When some of the smoke began to clear, Dau discovered that he and his fellow-invaders were surrounded by an army wearing Vizzglyth's livery, a very threatening army with very threatening weapons, many of them perched in a threatening manner atop a veritably terrifying steed. "Steed" in this instance does not necessarily signify a horse, for although there were ferociously frightening flashing black horses among their ranks, there were also a number of large animals which seemed a particularly unfriendly cross of lizard and bird. Like the warriors, some were green and some brown; unlike the warriors, some had scales, some feathers; however, these did not tend to grow in any apparent relationship to the semblances of other features, whether those tended towards the avian or the saurian. Some of the creatures drooled; others looked grimly thirsty, their tongues lolling though sharp-toothed grins.

Dau's instinct was to turn and run. Fear gripped him; he fought to hold on to conscious control of his body. Something tugged at his mind; he played tug-of-war with the grasping sensation, and eventually it went away. He looked around him; the air which had so recently seemed to hold an army of Vizzglyth's soldiers now betrayed no sign of them. Looking at his companions, he saw that most had remembered the Racklards' instructions. The others were eventually recalled to their senses.

The situation was at an impasse. Something had to give. The Racklards on both sides were getting pretty tired, for though their contest amounted to little more than a high-energy shoving match, yet both sides had to fight really hard just to stay where they were and not get shoved into the stratosphere by the power of the opponents' onslaught. Dau on the ground could close no more distance between his troop of troops and the barricades, as getting any closer to the wall would bring them within range of arrows which were already aimed.

*   *   *

"What's that over there!" yelled someone from one of Vizzglyth's watchtowers. Shouts of wonder soon echoed that cry, then echoed each other, as fingers pointed out a shape in the sky, a shape growing impossibly large as it neared. Larger than a cowherd, larger than a cow, large as a cowshed, a green, gold and yellow dragon flew towards the castle, an old man with a staff perched upon its back. This was an amazing spectacle in itself, but the formidable duo which now approached the castle with a singleminded purposefulness far more rapidly than any present had ever seen a cowshed fly had a look about them which made the defenders on the barricade shift uncomfortably where they stood.

As soon as he saw the castle barricade within range of his ferocious sneezes, Bahb Mawr Lei took a deep sniff from a particularly pollen-laden flower which he had brought along for the purpose. This immediately commenced ignition and the subsequent demolition of that structure, and this time the flames refused to be quenched as easily as those of the earlier fire had succumbed, so much the more because the dragon repeated the process a number of times to ensure that his purpose would fulfill itself.

*   *   *

When the watch sent up a cry that the castle was under attack by a dragon, the commanders therein finally saw fit to send out the real army, the one composed of real human soldiers. This army gathered just inside the castle gates, then burst forth with a loud battle cheer, fully two hundred sixty soldiers in full battle armor, marked as the vision army had been with Vizzglyth's symbolic House Buzzard. However, they rode no strange animals, and Dau had no mind struggle to overcome. Instead, once this army had crossed to the other side of the barricade, it stopped its charge and massed into a huddle. Its leaders conferred, then sent a messenger to Dau.

"Good day!" called this messenger as he ran up to Dau and the soldiers standing with him.

"Salutations," answered the warrior peasant.

"I represent the army you see, and speak as the messenger of the captains, who have taken a vote of the soldiers, the unanimous outcome of which was, that we would like to defect, and enlist in your army."

Dau was somewhat surprised by this abrupt speech. "Uh, thanks," he said. "I mean, that is, speaking on behalf of the assembled rebels as their tactical leader, we would greatly appreciate your help and support. In fact, your defection may be instrumental in the overthrow of the Emperor. And, uh, while we're talking about it, how about we start now with your army holding open that gate?"

At this point a knight in shining armor rode up, his visor down, with a lance in one hand. His shield bore a family crest with the words "Arthurus Pendragonus."

"I think you've got the wrong story, buddy," Dau growled to the knight errant. The figure on horseback seemed not to hear him, but continued to trot up to the castle. Then, to the surprise of all present, the knight disappeared. He didn't do it like the Racklards did it, all at once; his horse disappeared from nose to tail, and him on it, as if they had ridden through a door, a fact which entirely fit the explanation Aswelia gave of the event.

"He just rode through a rent in the space-time continuum," she said in an awed voice.

"The what?" said Dau.

"The... oh, it's a long story. It's like, the stuff that makes the universe seem linear, it gets weakened when a powerful surge of magical energy is concentrated in a single location. Apparently the Racklardian show-down was sufficient to actually put a hole in it."

"Wow."

*   *   *

In the interest of saving you lots of gory Hollywood details, I'll leave it all up to your imagination and just inform you that, with Dau at their head, a large army took Tlegryth's castle by storm and executed the false Emperor. Most of his Overlord cohorts who had helped him achieve his original conquest were killed; the rest were confined to the dungeons which had so recently contained today's victors.

The tide was turned on the Racklard battle. Some of the demigods fighting for Boovaus became so tired they forgot to sustain their immortality, and thus fell prey to rebel iron. So many of them succumbed to this blunder that soon their force was outnumbered and the battle lost.

The tortures inflicted in retribution by one set of excommunicated deities on another set would be more properly related in a proper mythology book. We omit the details here; but you may be certain it was something mythologically torturous.

Aaa

aaaaauuuuuuuu

auauauauauauauau

gggghhhhhhhhh!!!

Chapter 15: Victory Celebrations

That night around the campfire all were making merry. Many a soldier was whooping it up, drinking the wine Appletree had made from water, dancing with local girls: some of whom had received permission from their parents to stay out late; others of whom had slipped out the window after everybody else was in bed.

Racklardian minstrels, playing music of a style similar to that which the companions had heard in the hall under the Glatsflawn Mountains, piped and played on instruments unfamiliar to the locals. The songs they played were unfamiliar, but the music was groovy, and who could ask for anything more?

Everybody was dancing and having a good time. Well, everybody was having a good time; not everybody was dancing.

Dau Moth and Aswelia sat together underneath a tree, discussing how they should ask Appletree to take the position they had deemed him suitable to fill. The old man, no longer walking about invisible but greeted by all present as a hero, the man who had saved the day, was rigging up a strange apparatus with some help from Bahb Mawr Lei. It consisted of a number of short hollow tubes which pointed straight upwards, at the bottom of each of which he had attached a funny-smelling packet of some sort. Dau and Aswelia walked up behind the enchanter as he was running a fuse between the tubes in series, to an end which would remain a mystery to them until he lit one end of it.

"Uh, Appletree?" said Dau. "Can we talk to you?"

The magician looked up from his intent concentration, then smiled at the youngsters. "Why of course!" he beamed. "You'll have to excuse me for a minute, though, I'm almost done with this thing." He muttered to himself, stuck lengths of fuse in holes, tied a few knots and made some minor adjustments. Straightening up, or rather, standing up, for his back had not been quite straight for more than two hundred years, he glanced with a smile of satisfaction at his creation, which Dau now noticed covered some fifteen or twenty square feet with short tubes placed at regular intervals in a sort of star-shaped design. The tube at the center, which Appletree had just finished fidgeting with, was the tallest and fattest of the bunch. He pointed at this granddaddy tube, saying, "That's the grand finale. Just wait till you see it."

"What is it?" asked Aswelia, who had some inkling but wasn't really sure, having never before seen fireworks in real life.

"You'll find out," the mischievous magician replied airily. "Now, what did you want to talk to me about?"

The youths glanced at each other to decide who would do the speaking. Aswelia pointed at Dau; Mr. Hairball took this as a signal.

"We, ah, have a proposition for you." He glanced uncertainly at Aswelia, then continued thus. "Now that Vizzglyth is dead, somebody has to move into the castle to rule Tlegryth. Vizzglyth murdered the former King, who left no clear successor but a number of illegitimate children, none of whom has shown himself to be a particularly honorable or admirable character." He paused, searching for the right wording.

Dau could have been a writer, because when he had time to think of them, words came to him in a particularly artistic manner. However, he wasn't a writer, he was a farmer, and men who may have a talent for the pen are not necessarily also gifted orators. Placed in a situation where he had to think of something to say that sounded intelligent, Dau often found it simpler to not say anything at all and let someone else do the talking. However, as no "someone else" volunteered anything at this time, he continued.

"We were, like, thinking that you would be the ideal candidate for the job," he blurted. "So, uh, how would you like to be the King of Tlegryth?"

The smile fell off Appletree's face like an apple off a tree. "Me?" the magician asked, surprised. "Why would you want me to do it? I always assumed YOU would want to rule this country. This has been your battle since before I joined it, Dau Moth. Why don't want you want to be the King? All these people would back you up, for you're the man who just unseated a tyrant."

Dau looked flustered and looked from the magician to Aswelia, and back again. "But, you have to understand, long before I ever heard of this Overlord Vizzglyth fellow, I had a life that was going just fine, and a very reasonable plan about how I was going to spend the rest of it. I don't want all that changed. I just want to live out in the country with Aswelia. I want the stresses and worries in my life to be a direct result of nature's seasons, as those of a man of the fields must be. I couldn't adjust to living the life of politics, running back and forth against what everyone else thinks."

Appletree chuckled. "I suppose that is a problem. Young man, I don't want to do it for the very same reasons that you don't want to do it. I only ever wanted everything back as it was before the Overlords came: safe in someone else's hands. I am grateful for your offer, but the world of politics is not the life for me. I have no desire to spend my old age trying to influence other people, or worrying about how they influence me.

"If," the old man continued, "I were to interact with the masses of people in my later years (and you must agree with me that these days, all my years are my later years), I would choose a very different manner to go about it: more removed, yet somehow more direct. I would minister to their souls," he mused, "and teach them to focus their minds on kindness and happiness. No, my friends," he concluded, "my vegetable garden calls to me. Methinks I shan't tarry here much longer."

Dau was astounded. "But Appletree!" he protested. "Tlegryth needs your guidance! We all need you."

Appletree smiled and shook his head. "No," he said, turning to look at the soldiers and townsfolk reveling about the campfire, giving nary a mind to the somewhat gory mess they had left in the castle for someone else to clean up. "Look at these people. They don't need my guidance. They know how to live, and there's nothing more important than living. My guidance may be only good advice for myself; any who choose to follow it must have the option of realizing that. I could never force my will on someone else. Well, with the exception of what we just did to Vizzglyth, of course; but everyone makes exceptions sometimes," he chuckled. "My point is that the rules made by a government are actually in large part irrelevant to the lives led by the people. When the disparity gets too big, the people do what we just did to Vizzglyth. But that disparity always exists. What's important to realize is that the will to live is a powerful force, sufficient to keep the species alive, despite our most determined attempts to kill each other off." Appletree tugged on his beard and scratched his head. "On the other hand, I'm not proposing that we just leave the castle empty. It would be too easy for another Vizzglyth to invade and conquer."

"So do you think we should just destroy the building?" asked Dau doubtfully, looking at the forbidding fortress.

Bahb Mawr Lei couldn't suppress a chuckle at this idea. When Dau looked in his direction he burst into hysterics.

"Well, what's so funny?" demanded the human.

"Oh, I'm sorry I'm sorry I'm sorry," the dragon howled. It took him a minute to regain control of his vocal cords. "I suppose it would be possible, although certainly difficult. I wasn't laughing at the idea itself; it was the look on your face!" With that, the dragon burst into further irrelevant spasms of laughter. Dau decided the Rhasta dragon had probably drunk too much wine. Looking about to see if there was any evidence to support this conclusion, he noticed a 50 gallon water barrel, slightly charred at one end. Shaking his head, he looked to the magician, who, so far from seeming perturbed by his friend's behavior, was himself giving voice to an irrepressible chuckle.

"I must say I hadn't thought of that possibility," the wizard equivocated. "Well, ehem," he cleared his throat, "yes, tearing down the castle itself would solve the problem temporarily; but other castles can be built. The important thing is what the castle represents."

"What's that?" asked the attentive young man.

"Why, it's whatever the people want to think it represents," the old man answered with a glib tautology. "But, really, some sort of symbol to believe in and unite the people has been proven

effective for keeping out foreign invasions; and if
for no other reason, it's worth having just for that.
Besides, people seem to like that sort of thing."

"What about crime?" Dau demanded. His world
was falling apart with each new revelation.

"Oh, I suppose the economy has some effect on
crime, but no politicians yet have figured out how
to control the economy. No, politicians concern
themselves with the punishment of criminals a lot
more than they actually manage to cut down on
crime rates, and the punishment business is
certainly one I want no hand in."

Dau frowned. "Well, do you know what could
be done about crime, without the punishment?"

"Nothing can be done," the sorcerer replied
grimly. "That's the problem. People are like that:
they do horrible things to each other. There's
nothing any government can do about it, but it's the
reason governments exist in the first place. And
since we'll end up with a government one way or
another regardless, it's our responsibility to see
that one gets established here that will be, you
know, beneficial to us all, as much as possible: we,
the people; not warlords, authoritarians, or
degenerates." Appletree looked at him brightly.
"Eh? But no need to worry about that any more
tonight. Come, have a drink with me."

Appletree rummaged through the folds of his
cloak and produced, as if from nowhere, a bottle of
champagne. He popped the cork so that it hit his
gargantuan friend squarely on his enormous rump,

which caused the dragon to go into great gales of uproarious laughter for some minutes following.

Aswelia declined to have more than a taste, on account of her pregnancy; but the two men passed the bottle back and forth between them for some time.

Later on, in the middle of a lengthy discussion comparing dog breath with dragon breath, Appletree at no apparent provocation suddenly interrupted the conversation with a cry of, "Everybody look at the sky! It's time for the show!"

The wizard would respond to no questions but bustled over to his contraption. He bent over one side of it for a moment, then ran back from it as fast as he could.

A fuse burned up to the first of the cylinders, out of which burst a cloud of smoke and a ball of fire that flew into the air and exploded in a burst of colorful sparks high over their heads. A second burst of light followed, and a third; explosions started coming simultaneously, and two or three different bursts would appear in the sky at the same time.

All present marveled at the spectacle and cheered with each new display, as the explosions of light grew ever bigger and more colorful, climaxing with the granddaddy tube in the middle, which showed light bright as daylight on the surrounding countryside for some seconds.

"That was awesome, dude," Bahb Mawr Lei told Appletree appreciatively. The cheers of the hundreds assembled agreed with him for some time before finally everyone went back to their merrymaking.

Chapter 16: Journey to the Whett River

The next day at breakfast they began their conference, to look for a solution to the problem of who was to rule the country.

"We could go ask the Master Storyteller," Aswelia suggested.

"That's a great idea!" said Dau. "That way you can see the ocean like you said you wanted to. Surely, if he's the wisest person alive, his advice would be the best to follow."

Appletree offered no opinion. When pressed, he replied, "I must confess I have no superior strategy. If you really want to go visit the Master Storyteller, I will accompany you. I have not seen my old instructor in two centuries!" The old man went on to explain that the Master Storyteller was forty years his senior. "When I was twenty, sixty seemed really old," he joked. "I guess that makes the old codger three hundred forty years old! Fancy that."

"How is it that the two of you have grown so old, when all the world seeks elixirs of longevity?" asked Aswelia.

"In truth," the old man said, "it's mostly luck. However, we've both profited by that man's advice.

I was his pupil for perhaps three years, after I had completed my basic course at Enchanter's School. After that, I felt that I didn't need to be a student anymore; or at least, not a student whose course of instruction required the constant supervision of a human master. I have learned ever so much about the world since then, a lot of which I probably could have learned had I desired to undergo further instruction from a scholastic guide; but I feel that the experience of finding it out for myself was important to some extent. In those days he was known as Reigh Thael. I may not necessarily have been his favorite student, but I'm sure he will remember me. Still, I learned a lot from him, and to thank him for that I will accompany you on your visit."

*   *   *

The journey to the mouth of the Whett River took about two weeks at the leisurely pace at which they traveled, over the hilly but not difficult terrain. This journey was informative, in that they got to see a lot of the land and the people who lived in it. "I never knew Tlegryth was so big," Dau commented to Aswelia.

The Whett River delineated the northern border of Tlegryth and separated it from the northern countries which still resisted the rule of Emperor Vizzglyth and his Overlords. The companions journeyed overland on horseback, joining the Whett River near its mouth. Near the

coast they found a farmer with some fenced fields
for his other livestock who was willing to look after
their horses until they should come back for them.
He pointed them towards the ocean, saying it
wasn't far at all from where they were.

*   *   *

Their course intercepted the river just upriver
from its mouth, and they walked along its bank
downriver to the coast. The countryside here was
lightly forested; the verdant countryside was just
starting to show the evidence of too much August
sun, a sure sign that autumn would arrive in a
month or two. More or less. Seasons, of course,
refuse to abide by any sort of human calendar.
Coming around a bend, they suddenly found
themselves leaving the cover of the trees and
coming into a large, open space. Mounting a
hillock, they saw its other side stretching down a
wide sandy beach to an endless body of water.

"Oh, my God," said Aswelia.

"That's incredible," said Dau.

Appletree had seen the sea before, but he
hadn't really left Rendyll Forest much in the last
two hundred years, so he too was quite impressed
with the view. They were standing near the center
of the gentle curve of a huge crescent-shaped
expanse of beach, with nothing but driftwood,
seaweed, sand, seabirds and the occasional rock
visible for indeterminable miles on either side.
Almost in the center of this shallow bay was the

Whett River estuary; from their vantage point they could see a slight discoloration stretching out a little ways into the ocean where freshwater mingled with saltwater. They stood for some time in silence, absorbing the sight, until Aswelia started walking towards the breakers. Dau hesitated a moment, then followed her down the seashore. By the time he caught up with her she had already removed most of her clothes, placing them on a large driftwood log. Dau smiled at her bare breasts in the sunlight and the baby bulge just beginning to show beneath them. Taking off his own garments he suddenly realized just how exciting the mere sight of Aswelia's body was. She looked at him and shook her head. Grasping his erect member in one hand, she tugged on it gently.

"THIS is going to have to wait. I just wanted to go swimming," she said.

"That's okay," he said, smiling. "I, uh, I was just gonna go swimming, too. It's a hot day and the water looks inviting."

"Uh huh," she said skeptically.

"No, really! You just, uh," he leaned over and kissed her forehead and finished his sentence speaking into her hair, "turn me on without trying to."

"Well, then," she smiled, and spanked him saucily, "race you to the water!"

*   *   *

The ocean surf in which they played here was far more powerful than the little currents in the little creeks and pools they had played in as children, but as they were both able swimmers the extremism just made swimming more fun. Bodysurfing was a completely new concept to them, but they got quite a charge out of it. When they got out of the water for a rest and a snack, Appletree was nowhere to be seen, but just after they had donned their clothes and were lounging in the sun-warmed sand he appeared coming out of the trees, dragging a little rowboat behind him.

"Appletree!" Dau cried, jumping up to assist the elderly gentleman, "You should have gotten me out of the water! I would've helped you move that."

"Oh, no worries," said the magician. "'Tis not heavy at all."

Dau had now come to one side of the rowboat, which he grasped with one hand so Appletree wouldn't have to move it all by himself, and found to his amazement just how truly the magician spoke. Lifting the rowboat required little more effort than waving your hand at a soap bubble.

"But how is this?" puzzled the lad. "It looks and feels like wood, and as such should by rights weigh much more than I feel it to."

Appletree, walking backwards so as to simultaneously keep the boat moving and address his friend and student (for, you must admit that although Dau had enlisted in no class and wasn't doing any homework, he was sure learning a lot by hanging out with Appletree), affirmed that it was as wooden as any boat that would be made for centuries upon centuries to come. "It feels like it doesn't weigh a lot because I enlisted the aid of a column of air underneath it."

Dau saw now that there was a soft, blue green glow going all the way around the bottom of the boat, from wood to ground. "So, ah," he asked out of simple curiosity, "what happens if I do THIS?" and jumped into the boat, which sank instantly to the ground and ceased to budge with Appletree's tug on the rope.

"No, no, no," said the exasperated enchanter. "I have to rework the spell if you're going to do THAT."

Not wanting to get in anybody's way, Dau jumped out of the rowboat, a little bit embarrassed.

"So, where did you find it, Appletree?" queried Aswelia.

"Oh, it's courtesy of the Master Storyteller, who we're about to go visit. He leaves it out in plain view to assist the transportation of his visitors, but only those who already know him know how to see it."

"So, does he get a lot of visitors?"

"Ah, I'd say he probably doesn't. But you have to understand, this device isn't intended to discourage visitors, it's just so nobody walks off with his boat. Or, rather, rows off with it. He's really quite free with the secret of how to see it."

Setting the boat in the water, Dau took the oars. He hadn't really done a lot of rowing before, but Appletree explained it to him, and he got the hang of it without a lot of trouble, although he had the sneaking suspicion that the enchanter hadn't turned off that blue glow when the boat entered the water.

On the way to the island Appletree explained, "Storytelling in its higher sense is more than a repetition of the facts, like a brief blurb from the town crier on the evening news. Storytelling as an art form involves itself in the embellishment of those facts, with the purpose of making the story flow and the intent of making it interesting and even pleasing to the ear in the process. The Master Storyteller has perfected this art form."

Chapter 17: The Master Storyteller

The island on which the Master Storyteller Reigh Thael lived was almost rectangular, and took up what would have been about an acre of open sea, with almost a quarter of that space occupied by a completely out-of place gargantuan glacial erratic, sheer on all sides and uninviting to all save the avid rock climber, which none present were. The rest of the island was covered in a well-thinned but not actually logged woods, with what appeared to be dense vegetation, but which proved on closer examination to be a garden growing between the trees. The visitors tied their host's rowboat to a small dock next to a larger craft, a small sailboat just big enough for a sail, a covered cabin and enough deck to fish off.

"Well," said Appletree, "at least we can probably safely surmise that he's not out fishing, for he's not the sort who would own two fishing boats."

They walked up the dock into the trees. Though the island was not large and the woods were not dense, still it was difficult to see far in any direction. Branches and vines hanging from them obstructed vision, and the great unevenness of the ground further complicated any sort of visual search.

"He could be anywhere," observed Aswelia. "How are we supposed to find him?"

"I don't really know," admitted the wizard, "but I would suggest walking towards his house."

The Master Storyteller's abode was a fisherman's cottage located as far towards the far end of the island as one could walk, in a clearing between the trees and the towering singularity, quite near the large rock's abrupt face. The rock, towering over the structure which seemed dwarfed by the contrast, protected it from the nasty weather that sometimes blew in from the sea.

Appletree's hunch proved correct, for the wizened Reigh Thael was sitting in a comfortable chair on his front porch, drinking some tea and listening to the sunset, how the wind and birdsong and buzz of pesky biting insects changed as the great rock's afternoon shadow darkened his surroundings. He was a man of surprising proportions. Appletree had awarded him so much stature that the youngsters had simply assumed he would possess an unusual stature; indeed they had expected a very statue of a man. They had been given no real reason to expect this, so there's no reason to go on about it anymore. It may be interesting to the reader to note that, though he had been slightly taller as a young man, the Master Storyteller now measured four feet ten inches tall. Of course, he was less concerned about it than any other short human has ever been about his height.

In fact, during the course of their stay with him, it struck Dau that nothing flustered the Master; he always seemed relaxed and good-natured. His head was completely bald, but he had a long gray beard which he stroked sometimes while he was talking. He wore what looked like a bathrobe and wore no shoes on his leathery brown, wrinkled feet. What they didn't figure out until a while later was that he had extremely poor eyesight; cataracts in the days before laser surgery were quite difficult to treat. It was for this reason he walked with a cane, not as a mere aid to walking as Appletree used his staff.

"Good evening," he now called in a hoarse, friendly voice. He talked sort of like Uncle Remus in the movie Brer Rabbit, but I'm not going to try to imitate the writings of Mark Twain. When he spoke he closed his eyes and tilted his head to one side, sometimes changing the direction of the tilt with each new direction his thoughts took. "Who might I have the pleasure of greeting this glorious afternoon?"

"Sir, you would best remember me as T. C. App'yl Chtrae, though these youths know me as Appletree, to simplify the pronunciation," said the enchanter.

The Master Storyteller chuckled. "Appletree is it? Yes, that's a nice name to give yourself." He sipped his tea. "I haven't heard your voice in, oh, what is it now? Two hundred... fifty? Seventy years?"

"Two hundred seventy-five," the enchanter corrected.

"Ah, my old pupil, I see you still you still have a love for the exact. Oh, I'm glad you've come to visit. It's so nice to have visitors. I try not to fall into a routine, but when you've spent a certain number of years all by yourself on a small island, it is difficult to not notice some sort of pattern in your movements. And who are these tadpoles you've brought with you, my friend the bullfrog?"

Dau was a bit surprised to hear himself referred to as a legless baby amphibian, but Appletree laughed out loud at being called a bullfrog. "These are my friends, Dau Moth and Aswelia. These two young people were recently instrumental in the overthrow of the Overlord Vizzglyth. I don't know how much you keep up with politics."

"I have heard of this Vizzglyth, who declared himself Emperor and started pillaging and burning. I was not aware that his rule had ended. That's good news. And you two were instrumental in his overthrow, eh? Wonderful, wonderful. I'm pleased to meet you. You said your names were Aswelia and Dau Moth? Wonderful, wonderful," he repeated. "Please, call me Reigh Thael."

"Nice to meet you," the youngsters each said in turn, shaking the guru's hand. Both of the youngsters had but to spend a matter of minutes with him before deciding that he was unquestionably a vibrant, vivacious person, full of those qualities which lent authority to whatever answer he might make to their questions.

"We've come to ask you..." Aswelia started.

"Oh, I'm sure you have," their host interrupted, "but it can wait until after dinner, can't it?"

Somewhat taken aback, Aswelia fell silent.

"It'll just take a minute to cook up," said the Master Storyteller, who made no move to start fixing it, but took another sip of his tea, rocked back and forth in his chair and smiled to himself. "So, my former student, how have you made out?"

After Appletree described his long years of solo research in the woods, his old master chuckled. "You always were a loner, Appletree," the Master Storyteller remarked, "working best by yourself. Well, I suppose I understand; look at me, a hermit on his island. Almost like Yoda," he mused, a reference which made no sense at all to either of the youngsters. The former teacher and student talked at length about old days, a fascinating conversation to both of the youngsters, neither of whom said much during its course. Finally the hermit invited them all inside, promising dinner would be ready soon. "You just had the good fortune to arrive on the day when I was cooking myself enough food for the next three days, so there should be enough to feed four."

It was a simple little shack. Dau was impressed with its inherent sense of balance, with neither too many nor two few rooms, just the right amount of clutter to make the place feel lived in but not enough mess to make the housekeeper seem like a packrat. Here and there in odd places around the rooms were figurines and abstract sculptures the Master Storyteller had whittled from driftwood, surely a difficult accomplishment for someone who couldn't see the knife.

There was, indeed, more than enough food for four, and homebrew to go with it.

"This is the second-tastiest drink we have enjoyed on our entire journey," Appletree complimented him.

"Only the second?" the Storyteller asked with an amused smile and a cocked eyebrow.

"There is really nothing in the whole world to rival the Ambrosia of the demigods," the wizard explained.

"Ah," said the Master Storyteller, and enjoyed another sip. "Well, if you're comparing my homebrew to Ambrosia, then I take it that I'm doing something right."

"You are," Aswelia assured him.

"You most certainly are," Dau agreed.

After the meal had been served and the four of them were sitting in a circle on the floor around a loaf of bread and a pot of soup, Aswelia again brought up her question to the Master Storyteller. She explained the problem of the succession, just as Dau had explained it to Appletree.

Reigh Thael nodded. He ruminated for some moments, then began an interrogative interview with the young couple, asking them extensive and detailed questions. He had them describe the battle, the other soldiers, and their feelings towards all sorts of things. At length, after more rumination, he began to expostulate. His full dissertation took him upwards of an hour and a half to deliver, much of that time spent in telling the full-length version of the following fish story.

*   *   *

The words of the Master Storyteller were never set down in print, so no direct record exists of exactly what he said. We are told by the historians of Tlegryth that few people have ever even approached the Master Storyteller's genius for oration. It seems certain that his words were so well-chosen and his tales so masterfully told that it is beyond this writer's ability to attempt to retell them. Any attempt at plot summary would trivialize the stories unforgivably.

Nonetheless, I shall attempt to tell you what the Master Storyteller told our heroes; but please understand, dear reader, that this is a mere summary; and if I make it sound childish and pointless, that is a failing of the present scribe, not the original Master Storyteller; for when he told this tale, it was deep, eloquent, charming, funny, sad, and poetic.

Chapter 18: The Tale
of Harold the Trout

Once upon a time there was a trout named Harold. Harold the trout was searching for the perfect mate. He didn't want to spawn with just anybody: he wanted his lady trout to be nothing short of perfection itself.

Now, at the time, Harold had been dating a very nice, very pretty trout named Betsy, but he didn't want to just settle for a girl from his home stream. He figured the river system must be full of fish, and somewhere out there was a delicately finned creature much more perfect than Betsy. So one day, he set off without even telling her that he was leaving.

So Harold the trout went exploring. It was true, there were many other fish in the river system. He traveled up one stream and down another; there's a lot of land that can be covered in this manner. His hypothesis proved correct, or so it seemed at first. Around every river bend, hiding beneath a thousand little rocks, a thousand eroded banks, and innumerable tree roots, were a thousand female trout, each more gorgeous than the last. He didn't

want to choose one too quickly, without seeing a lot
of them; so he swam farther and farther,
continually amazed by the beauty of the troutesses
he swam past. (Picture here, if you will, a cartoon
animation of a grinning, Hollywood-handsome buff
male trout, swimming against the current past a
drop-dead knockout gorgeous female trout who is
demurely drifting in a pool on one side of the river.
He keeps swimming, but turns his head to stare at
her as he goes by. Not looking where he's going, he
runs headfirst into a rock.)

After he had seen quite a few uncommonly
good-looking troutesses, Harold began to grow
insensitive to them. Although many of them were
such attractive specimens that any local trout
would have swooned for them, still he continued his
search unsatisfied, always convinced that just
around the next bend lay a fish more perfect than
the last.

When Harold finally did try to get to know
some of the attractive trouts he met along his long
travels, he found his difficulties in his search for
perfection multiplied. Some were too needy, some
too overbearing, some too distant. Many of them
were so fully conscious of their beauty that they
considered it their badge of superiority, and in their
unbearable haughtiness, they wouldn't deign to
speak to almost anybody. Others had learned to use
their good looks to their advantage, getting favors
from others and giving nothing back in return.
Some took this latter behavior to an extreme, and
were really quite cruel to those who had the

misfortune to find them attractive. And an astounding number were, though spectacularly visually appealing, so *frog-brained* as to be uninteresting to talk to and a total bore to try to spend time with.

Harold began to despair of ever finding a perfect mate.

Finally, one day Harold said to himself, "I give up. I'll never find the perfect fish for me. I guess I'll just enjoy the rest of my life as a bachelor."

Having put the whole matter out of his mind as useless and pointless, he rounded a corner in the river; and there he observed a trout whose beauty struck him: even he, who had become hardened to the wiles of women after seeing so many attractive lady-trouts, was astounded by her amazing grace and beauty.

Harold hesitated not a moment, but swam right up to her, saying, "I have swum this river system for miles and miles, and you are the most beautiful trout I have seen in my travels."

"Really?" she said. "Why, thank you, that's really sweet."

"Pray tell, my lady," he asked, "what is thy name?"

"Why, Harold," the beautiful trout asked in startled surprise, "don't you remember me?"

Harold was astounded. Could it truly be that he had met this trout before, and foolishly passed her up? He wondered what fault he had found with her. She seemed to be perfect in every way.

"I'm Betsy," she finished, sounding rather cross. "Where in the world have you been?"

Chapter 19: Happily Ever After

Dau wondered how appropriate it would be to exchange significant glances with Aswelia at this point. She wondered the same thing. Eventually both found it irresistible. But that wasn't the Master Storyteller's point.

"So, sometimes the best options are the really obvious ones that are so blatant you don't even realize that they're options," Appletree summed up for his former Master. "She was there all along."

"And Harold the trout was a total asshole," remarked astute Aswelia, "who abandoned the perfect girlfriend for no good reason, just because he wanted to play the field. I hope she doesn't take him back; or if she does, I hope she makes him pay."

The problem with that fishy story, thought Dau privately, *is that I don't wholeheartedly agree with its moral. Yes, there are certainly cases when the best of the lot is right under your nose; but in other cases, one is sometimes compelled by circumstances to keep looking indefinitely.* He wisely did not give voice to this train of thought, wishing to avoid a confrontation with the beautiful Aswelia. *I guess the Master Storyteller is a mischievous old bugger, subtly loading the moral of his story with a point of view that might seem to encourage a certain sort of behavior. He might have chosen a less roundabout way to give advice. However, we mustn't question the wisdom of the wise, for we have more important tasks to take in hand.*

"It sounds to me," Reigh Thael the Master Storyteller said then, "as though the army that helped you to overthrow Vizzglyth is full of men qualified for the job. I'm sure you can think of a man who's intelligent, capable, honest, and well liked by the company."

Thinking about this for a moment, Dau and Aswelia both replied that there was a man named Lieutenant Froth who had all those qualifications and more.

"Is he qualified to be the King of Tlegryth?" asked Reigh Thael.

All three visitors agreed that he was.

"You've helped us so much!" said Aswelia. "How can we ever thank you enough?"

"But I didn't do anything," protested the Master Storyteller. "I just helped you to see what you already knew. When the three of you put your heads together, you all agreed. You already knew who the best candidate for the job was, you just had to allow yourselves to realize that you knew it."

They admitted that this was so.

Appletree, Aswelia, and Dau spent the night at Reigh Thael's house. He told them many tales in that time, spun theories and philosophized on all sorts of subjects. He really was an amazing fellow.

When it was time for his three visitors to leave, the Master Storyteller solemnly shook the hand of each.

"Your visit has made me reflect," the Master Story said in parting. Then he turned around three times, with his head tilted so far to one side that his ear was almost touching his shoulder. "Always a teacher, always a student," he continued, without explaining his oddly erratic behavior. He held an expostulatory finger in he air. "I am now giving myself a new assignment. I recommend it to you as well, my friend T. C., though of course you are under no pressure or obligation.

"I have just realized how little interaction I've had with people," the Storyteller continued. "Why, I think it's been almost seven years since the last time I had a human visitor! I don't know if it's because we're male, or because we're intelligent, or perhaps some combination of the two, but Appletree, we don't interact well with other people, you and I. My next assignment, to try to broaden my horizons, is to go out into the world and learn how to get along with people. I suddenly think I've rather been avoiding it all my life. Well, may the Force be with you."

He waved his walking-stick in the air and turned around, tapping the ground with it as he hobbled back to his hut.

*   *   *

After returning to the castle, Dau made a speech to the assembled troops and townspeople, nominating Froth to be the new leader of the land.

The majority of the assembled people cheered their assent. At Appletree's suggestion, they hastily organized a vote. Everyone present cast a pebble in one or another of a series of vases. When the stones were counted, they were overjoyed to see that the motion had been carried. The rather surprised Lieutenant Froth, now a King when such a notion had never really crossed his mind, made another speech, promising to make the best of their good faith, and nominating Grebron Auroyon as his chief advisor.

*   *   *

And they all lived happily ever after.

The reader may rest assured that "living happily ever after" does not indicate a life free of trouble or problems. It is the nature of things to go in cycles of better, worse, better, worse; and sometimes the 'worse' part of the cycle seems to take up more than its fair share of time.

Still, Dau Moth, Aswelia, and all their friends had gained valuable insights during their struggle against the Overlords. Having fought for their freedom, they valued it all the more. Having nearly lost their lives, they became aware of how precious life is.

Thus, when at times the harvest was poor, or the well ran dry, or the fences needed mending, or

the deer and rabbits plundered the vegetable
garden; even when in-laws stopped over for dinner
unannounced at entirely the wrong moment: the
loving young couple could take a deep breath and
grin.

And then they had kids.

The End